OFF THE MAT

NIKI ROBINSON AGUE

1

Muddy Water

Stop stirring. Be still. Clarity will come on its own.

The door opened at 9:07.

Maeve didn't look up. She'd been mid-sentence, guiding twenty-three bodies into stillness, her voice low and steady in the heated room. She heard the familiar sounds anyway: the soft thud of a bag hitting the floor, the whisper of a mat unrolling, the crinkle of someone settling into place while everyone else held their breath. Not because she'd told them to.

Diane. It was always Diane.

Seven minutes late to a class about stillness. There was a poem in that somewhere, if Maeve weren't so tired to find it.

She continued without pause. She had been in the

middle of an opening breath work sequence. Margaret in the front left corner, where she'd been every Tuesday for eleven years. The new woman in the back, fourth class now, still rigid with the effort of trying to relax. Kyle, the former triathlete who treated every pose like a race he was losing.

And Diane, finally still, already forgiven. That was the thing about Diane—you couldn't stay mad at her. She arrived late to everything, apologized to no one, and somehow filled whatever room she entered with a warmth that made the disruption feel almost worth it.

"Before we move, I want to tell you a story." Maeve continued.

She let the silence build. This was the part she loved —the moment before the teaching, when the room became a held breath. Twenty-three people waiting. The infrared heaters humming their low frequency. The smell of eucalyptus and clean sweat.

"There was a student," she began, "who came to a Zen master in a state of agitation. His mind wouldn't stop churning. Thoughts everywhere—worries, plans, regrets. He asked the master: How do I find peace? How do I make it stop?"

She paused. Somewhere in the room, someone's stomach growled. She didn't react.

"The master pointed to a glass of water on the table. It was murky, full of sediment. He asked the student: What do you see?"

"Muddy water," she continued. "The student said he couldn't see through it. So the master told him to watch.

And they sat. In silence. For several minutes. Just watching the glass."

Maeve opened her own eyes now, scanning the room. Some students had their eyes closed, listening. Others watched her. Kyle was already fidgeting, adjusting his position. The Weeper—that's what Maeve privately called her, the woman going through a divorce who cried in every hip opener—sat perfectly still, tears already tracking down her cheeks. The story hadn't even landed yet. Her body just knew what was coming.

"Slowly," Maeve said, "the sediment began to settle. The mud drifted to the bottom. The water grew clear. And the master said: You didn't have to do anything to the water. You didn't have to filter it or fix it. You simply had to stop stirring it. Your mind is the same. Stop stirring. Be still. Clarity will come on its own."

She let that sit.

"Tonight," she said, "we practice being the glass. We don't force the mud to settle. We create the conditions for settling to happen. We bring this practice to the spine—the central channel of our being."

They moved into Caterpillar—a forward fold, the whole back body gently stressed. Maeve walked the room, adjusting, offering bolsters. "Let your head hang heavy," she said. "In this pose, we're not trying to touch our toes. We're not trying to do anything. We're creating stillness in the body so the sediment can settle."

She paused beside Margaret, the eleven-year regular

who still set up facing the wrong direction half the time. Margaret, who had buried her husband three years ago and came to class the following Tuesday like nothing had happened. Who had never once mentioned it. Who folded into Caterpillar now with the same quiet determination she brought to everything.

"Your mind may feel like muddy water right now," Maeve continued, moving through the room. "That's okay. You don't need to fix it. Just stop stirring."

She found herself by the Weeper, whose tears had intensified. The woman was folded over, shaking slightly, trying to be silent about it. Maeve knelt beside her.

"That's it," she whispered, so quiet only the woman could hear. "Let it move through."

The woman nodded, eyes still closed, tears still falling. Maeve moved on.

They moved through the sequence—Sphinx, then Seal for those who wanted deeper. Twisted Roots on both sides, the spine rotating, wringing out. Dragonfly, a wide-legged fold that opened everything. Through each pose, Maeve returned to the teaching.

"Notice when you start stirring," she said during a long hold. "The urge to adjust. The mental math of how much longer. The story about whether you're doing it right. That's all stirring. See if you can just... stop."

Kyle adjusted his position for the fourteenth time. She saw it in her peripheral vision but didn't call it out.

Some people had to learn the hard way that stillness couldn't be won.

By the time they reached savasana, the room had changed. It always did. Something about an hour of stillness in heat—it broke people down, softened them. The air felt different. Heavier. Sacred, even, if you believed in that sort of thing.

Maeve did believe. After fifteen years, she still believed.

"Let yourself be the glass," she said, her voice barely above a whisper now. "You don't have to fix anything. You don't have to solve anything. The mud will settle on its own if you just... stop... stirring."

Silence. The heaters hummed. Someone breathed deeply. In the back corner, the new woman had finally unclenched her jaw.

Maeve closed her own eyes. For just a moment, she let herself rest too. Let the mud settle. Let the water clear.

Then her phone buzzed in her bag across the room.

She ignored it. Held the silence. But somewhere in her chest, the stirring had already begun.

* * *

The phone call was from Finn's school.

He'd bitten someone. Again.

Maeve stood in the studio's back room, still in her teaching clothes, sweat cooling on her skin while the assistant principal explained the situation with the practiced patience of a woman who had delivered this kind of news many times before. Finn had been in the block corner. Another child had taken a block he wanted. Words were exchanged—well, words on the other child's part; Finn's vocabulary was still catching up to his emotions. And then teeth met forearm.

"He broke the skin this time, Mrs. Cambell," the assistant principal said. "The other child's parents are understandably upset."

Maeve leaned against the wall and closed her eyes. Stop stirring, she told herself. Let the mud settle.

"I'll be there in twenty minutes," she said.

She drove the familiar route from the studio to the school, her mind churning despite her best efforts. The tuition for this school—the school that was supposed to be better equipped for spirited children, that was supposed to understand that some five-year-olds just had more weather inside them—was $1,800 a month. Times three schools, because Sage was in high school now and Eli was at the middle school, and somehow Maeve and James had decided years ago that private education was worth the constant low-grade financial terror.

$5,400 a month. Just in tuition. Not counting

uniforms, supplies, field trips, the endless fundraising asks.

She thought about the class she'd just taught. The parable. The muddy water.

You didn't have to filter it or fix it.

But Finn kept biting people. And the tuition was due next week. And somewhere in her inbox was an email from Sage's teacher about a missing assignment, and another from Eli's counselor asking to schedule a meeting—Eli, her sweet middle child who never asked for anything and therefore often got nothing—and James had texted this morning asking if she'd thought more about the conversation they'd started last night, the one about whether they were okay, really okay, or just going through the motions of a marriage.

Stop stirring.

She couldn't stop stirring. The spoon was attached to her hand.

Finn was in the office when she arrived, sitting on a chair designed for someone twice his size, his feet dangling above the floor. He looked impossibly small. Also unrepentant. His face, when he saw her, shifted through several emotions in quick succession: relief, then defiance, then something that might have been shame but got swallowed before it could fully form.

"He took my block," Finn said immediately.

"I know," Maeve said. She knelt in front of him so

they were eye to eye. "But we don't bite, remember? We use our words."

"I don't have enough words," Finn said. And the thing was, he wasn't being difficult. He was being accurate. At five, Finn experienced emotions at a volume his vocabulary couldn't match. The gap between what he felt and what he could express came out through his body—through thrown objects, through screams, through teeth.

Maeve understood this. She also understood that understanding didn't matter to the parents of the child with the bite mark on his arm.

"Then we find other ways," she said. "We walk away. We find a teacher. We take deep breaths." She demonstrated, exaggerating the inhale. "Like this, remember? In through the nose—"

"I know how to breathe," Finn snapped. "Breathing doesn't get my block back."

She almost laughed. Would have, if the assistant principal weren't watching from behind her desk, if the stakes weren't what they were. Finn had just articulated something most adults couldn't name: the insufficiency of all the tools she offered. Breathing doesn't solve the problem. Stillness doesn't pay the bills. Meditation doesn't make the biting stop.

"You're right," she said quietly. "Breathing doesn't get the block back. But biting doesn't either. And now you're in trouble, and the other boy is hurt, and neither of you has the block."

Finn considered this. His face worked through the logic. Finally, reluctantly: "Can we go home now?"

"Yes," Maeve said. "We can go home."

* * *

Home was chaos.

The dogs needed out the moment she walked in—Kona, the old lab mix who'd been with her since before any of the children existed; Mochi, the anxious golden who'd been a pandemic puppy and still hadn't fully recovered from the lack of early socialization; and Beans, the new one, a four-month-old mutt who chewed everything and peed when excited, which was always.

"Stay here," she told Finn, depositing him in front of the TV—screen time limits be damned—while she wrestled three leashes onto three dogs and stumbled out the back door.

The yard was small. The dogs circled it anyway, performing their elaborate sniffing rituals. Maeve stood in the middle and let them orbit her, her mind still churning.

Stop stirring.

She couldn't stop.

The assistant principal's words cycled through her head.

This is the third incident this month. We need to see improvement, or we'll have to discuss other options.

Other options. The phrase was a knife wrapped in cotton. It meant: fix your child, or we'll ask him to leave.

And beneath that, the darker current: What kind of mother raises a child who bites? What kind of yoga teacher talks about peace and stillness while her own son is drawing blood on the playground? What kind of fraud stands in front of a room full of people and teaches lessons she can't live herself?

Kona nudged her hand. Maeve looked down at the old dog—gray around the muzzle now, slower than she used to be, but still present. Still showing up.

"I know," Maeve said. "I know."

The afternoon blurred into evening the way it always did—a series of tasks completed without memory of completing them. Snacks procured. Homework supervised. Eli's quiet return from school, his "fine" when she asked how his day was, the way he disappeared into his room with his book and didn't emerge until dinner.

She should have knocked. Should have sat on his bed and asked real questions—not "how was school" but "what made you laugh today" or "what was hard" or "is there anything you need that you're not asking for?"

She didn't. There wasn't time. Finn needed redirection away from the TV. The dogs needed feeding. Dinner needed to happen. James would be home at 6:30, and the table should be ready, and somewhere in all of it she'd lost track of the fact that her middle child was becoming invisible in his own house.

Sage arrived at 5:45, dropped off by a friend's mother after volleyball practice. She stormed through the door in that particular way of fourteen-year-old girls—all drama and eye rolls and energy that filled the room like weather.

"Can I go to Maya's this weekend?" she demanded, before even removing her shoes.

"Hello to you too," Maeve said, stirring something on the stove.

"Hi. Can I?"

"I don't know. I'd have to talk to her parents. What's happening at Maya's?"

"Nothing. Just hanging out."

"All weekend?"

"God, Mom. It's not a big deal."

It probably wasn't. But Maeve was tired, and the school had called, and James's text from this morning was still unanswered, and somewhere in her body the stirring had become a churning, sediment swirling so thick she couldn't see through to anything.

"I said I'd have to think about it," she snapped. "Go wash your hands for dinner."

Sage's face shifted—hurt flashing before the armor went up. "Fine," she said, cold now. "Whatever." She disappeared upstairs, footsteps loud on purpose.

Maeve gripped the spoon. Felt the heat of the stove. Wanted to throw something.

Stop stirring.

She kept stirring.

. . .

James walked in at 6:32. Two minutes late, which shouldn't have mattered but did—not because of the two minutes themselves but because of everything they represented. The meetings that ran over. The traffic he couldn't control. The hundred small ways life conspired to keep him from being where she needed him, when she needed him, even though she knew—she *knew*—it wasn't his fault.

"Hey," he said, dropping his bag by the door. "Smells good."

"Finn bit someone again."

She hadn't meant to open with that. Hadn't meant her voice to sound like that—flat and accusatory, as if it were James's fault, as if their son's teeth in another child's arm were somehow a failure of fatherhood.

James's face did something complicated. Concern, frustration, and something that might have been exhaustion—not with Finn, but with the way this news was being delivered. With her.

"Is he okay?" James asked.

"He's fine. The other kid needed a bandage."

"Where is he?"

"Living room. I let him watch TV." She heard the defensiveness in her own voice, the preemptive strike against judgment that hadn't been offered. "I needed to make dinner."

James didn't say anything. Just nodded, set down his bag properly, and went to find his son.

Maeve stood alone in the kitchen, stirring a pot of

something she couldn't taste, feeling the sediment swirl and swirl and swirl.

Dinner was what it always was: barely controlled chaos. Finn refused to eat anything except the rice, and only after confirming it wasn't touching anything else on the plate. Eli answered questions in monosyllables, his book visible in his lap under the table. Sage maintained a pointed silence that radiated disapproval across the whole room. James tried to make conversation about his day; Maeve tried to listen; neither quite succeeded.

"How was class?" James asked her, when the silence grew too heavy.

"Good," she said. "We did a yin sequence. Spine focus."

"What was the theme?"

He always asked. After fifteen years, he still asked. It was one of the ways he showed up—not understanding her world but being curious about it. Making space for it.

"Muddy water," she said. "The Zen story about not stirring."

"Tell me."

She hesitated. The kids were half-listening now—even Sage, despite herself. Maeve told the story again, abbreviated. The student and the master. The glass of murky water. The waiting. The settling.

Stop stirring. Clarity will come on its own.

When she finished, Finn said: "That's stupid."

"Finn," James warned.

"It is! If the water's muddy, you pour it out and get new water."

Maeve opened her mouth to correct him, to explain the metaphor, to teach the lesson she was supposed to teach. But something stopped her. She looked at her five-year-old son—this child of pure will and insufficient words, who solved problems with his teeth because his vocabulary couldn't keep up with his experience—and she thought:

Maybe he's right.

Maybe sometimes you couldn't just wait for the mud to settle. Maybe sometimes the water was too thick, the sediment too stirred, and the only option was to start over. Pour it out. Get new water.

But that wasn't how life worked, was it? You couldn't pour out your children. Your marriage. Your financial obligations. Your own churning mind.

You had to work with the water you had.

The evening unwound in its usual rhythm. Finn's bath. The negotiation over toothbrushing. The three stories that became five because he knew exactly how to ask. James handled most of it—he was good at bedtime, patient in ways Maeve couldn't be by that hour—while she cleaned the kitchen, loaded the dishwasher, wiped the counters, fed the dogs again because Beans had knocked over his bowl.

Eli drifted past on his way to his room. "Night, Mom."

"Wait." Maeve caught his arm. He stopped, surprised. "How are you? Really."

Eli considered the question. He was so careful with his words, this child—so thoughtful, so unlike his brother in every way.

"I'm okay," he said. Then, quieter: "I finished my book today."

"Which one?"

"The one about the kid who survives on the island."

"Did you like it?"

A small smile. "It was good. He learned to make fire."

Maeve pulled him into a hug. He let her, for a moment. Then squirmed away—too old for this, but not quite.

"I'm glad you're okay," she said. "I'm sorry I didn't ask earlier."

Eli shrugged. "It's fine. You were busy."

He disappeared into his room, and Maeve stood in the hallway, the weight of *it's fine, you were busy* pressing on her chest like a stone.

She found Sage at 9:15, as she did every night. Knocked on the door. Waited.

"Come in."

The room was dark except for fairy lights strung along the ceiling—a remnant of Sage's younger self, the one who still believed in magic. Maeve sat on the edge of the bed. Her daughter was a shadow under the covers, face barely visible.

"I'm sorry about earlier," Maeve said. "About Maya's. I was stressed and I took it out on you."

Sage was quiet for a moment. Then: "Finn bit someone again?"

"Yeah."

"He's such a weirdo."

"Don't call your brother a weirdo."

"He's literally biting people, Mom. That's weird."

Maeve couldn't argue with the logic. "He's having a hard time. His feelings are big and his words are small."

Sage turned to face her in the dark. Maeve could barely see her expression, but she felt it—the shift from irritation to something softer.

"That's kind of like what you teach, isn't it?" Sage said. "The feelings thing."

"What do you mean?"

"I don't know." A pause. "Just... sometimes I think about the stuff you used to tell me when I was little. When we did yoga together. About how feelings are like waves. They come and they go."

Maeve's throat tightened. This girl—this teenage girl who rolled her eyes at yoga and claimed her mother was embarrassing—remembered.

"You remember that?"

"I remember everything," Sage said. Then, quieter: "I just don't like to show it."

Maeve reached out and found her daughter's hand in the dark. Sage let her hold it.

"You can go to Maya's," Maeve said. "If her parents say it's okay."

"Really?"

"Really."

A small squeeze of her hand. "Thanks, Mom."

They sat like that for a while—mother and daughter, in the dark, in the quiet. Outside the fairy lights, the world kept churning. But in here, just for a moment, the mud was settling.

* * *

It was nearly ten when Maeve finally sat down.

The house was quiet. James was in bed, not asleep but waiting—she knew the particular quality of his waiting, the way it filled a room. The dogs were settled in their various spots: Kona on her bed by the door, Mochi on the couch she wasn't supposed to be on, Beans in his crate, finally still.

Maeve sat in the living room, lights off, and did something she hadn't done all day.

She stopped.

Not stopped moving—she'd done that. But stopped stirring. Stopped the mental churning, the rehearsal of conversations, the calculation of tuition costs, the replay of Finn's face in the principal's office, Sage's hurt expression, Eli's *it's fine, you were busy*.

She just sat. And watched.

The sediment began to settle.

Not all of it. Not completely. But enough to see

through to something underneath. A truth she'd been avoiding.

She was tired. Bone tired. Soul tired. The kind of tired that didn't get fixed by sleep because it wasn't about sleep—it was about the constant pouring of herself into everything and everyone, the daily emptying that never quite got refilled.

And she was doing it to herself.

The stirring—it wasn't life doing it to her. It was her, spoon in hand, churning the water because she didn't know how to stop. Because stopping felt like failing. Because if she wasn't actively fixing everything, wasn't the water just getting muddier?

But no. That wasn't how it worked. The whole point of the story—the point she'd taught that morning and promptly forgotten—was that the fixing was the problem. The stirring was what kept the mud suspended.

You didn't have to filter it or fix it. You simply had to stop stirring it.

Maeve sat in the dark for a long time. The house breathed around her. The dogs snored. The refrigerator hummed. And slowly, slowly, the water began to clear.

She couldn't solve Finn's biting in this moment. Couldn't pay the tuition, repair whatever was fraying between her and James, give Eli the attention he deserved, or bridge the gap with Sage. But she could stop pretending that churning on all of it would help.

She could put down the spoon.

She could let the mud settle.

She could trust that clarity would come—not

because she forced it, but because that's what clarity did when you got out of its way.

When she finally went to bed, James was still awake. He reached for her in the dark, and she let him pull her close.

"Long day?" he asked.

"Yeah."

"Want to talk about it?"

She thought about it. About the text he'd sent this morning, still unanswered. About the question underneath it:

Are we okay? Really okay?

"Not tonight," she said. "But soon. Can we talk soon?"

He was quiet for a moment. Then: "Yeah. Soon."

She pressed her face into his shoulder. Let herself be held. Let the mud settle, just a little more.

Tomorrow the water would get stirred again. Finn would refuse breakfast. Sage would need something signed. Eli would disappear into his book. There would be bills and emails and the endless negotiation of keeping a family afloat.

But tonight, in the dark, in the quiet, Maeve practiced what she preached.

She stopped stirring.

She let the clarity come.

And just before sleep took her, she thought of something Finn had said at dinner:

If the water's muddy, you pour it out and get new water.

Maybe. Maybe sometimes you did.

But sometimes—maybe most of the time—you just had to trust the settling. Trust that the mud would find the bottom. Trust that the water would clear.

Trust that you didn't have to fix everything to be okay.

You just had to stop stirring long enough to see.

2

The Second Arrow
Pain is inevitable. Suffering is optional.

The Buddha once told a story about two arrows.

Maeve stood at the front of the room, Tuesday morning, 9 a.m., twenty-six students arranged on their mats like a geometry problem. Hips today. The sequence would be long holds, deep openings, the kind of class that made people cry or fall asleep or both.

"When we experience something painful," she said, "that's the first arrow. It hits us. We didn't ask for it. We couldn't avoid it. It just... landed."

She paused, letting the words settle.

"But then we do something interesting. We pick up a second arrow and shoot ourselves with it. The pain was bad enough—but now we add suffering on top. We add the story about the pain. The judgment. The 'why me.' The 'I should be handling this better.' The 'what's wrong with me that this hurts so much.'"

In the front row, a woman nodded. She came every Tuesday. Maeve didn't know her story, but she knew the nod—the recognition of someone who had shot herself with many arrows.

"The Buddha's teaching is this: we can't always control the first arrow. But the second arrow? That one's optional. That one we choose."

She gestured toward the mats. "Today, in these long holds, you're going to feel sensation. That's the first arrow—it's just information from your body. Watch what happens next. Watch the second arrows fly. 'I hate this pose.' 'I'm not flexible enough.' 'Everyone else is deeper than me.' 'When will this be over.' Those are all second arrows. See if you can feel the first arrow without adding the second."

They moved into Butterfly, the soles of the feet together, knees wide. Five minutes. Maeve walked the room.

"The goal isn't to feel nothing," she said. "The goal is to feel what's actually happening—without adding a story about what it means."

.

The class unfolded the way yin classes do—slowly, quietly, with occasional sighs and one woman who fell asleep in Sleeping Swan and snored gently until Maeve touched her shoulder. They moved through Dragon, through Half Saddle, through Sphinx. Each pose a container for sensation. Each hold an opportunity to watch the mind reach for its arrows.

"Notice," Maeve said during a long Dragonfly hold, legs wide, torso folded forward. "Notice when you want to fix something. Adjust. Escape. That impulse—that's the hand reaching for the second arrow. See if you can just... not pick it up."

She said the words and meant them.

She also knew that approximately two hours ago, she had shot herself with more arrows than she could count.

* * *

The morning started at 4:47 a.m., thirteen minutes before her alarm, when Finn's foot connected with her chest.

He slept like a clock. That was the only way to describe it—every hour, his body rotated. He'd start the night perpendicular, head on James's pillow, feet toward Maeve. By midnight he'd be diagonal. By 2 a.m., fully horizontal, a human barrier between his parents. By 4:47, his feet were on her sternum, small toes pressing into her collarbone, his head hanging off James's side of the bed.

First arrow: foot to chest.

Second arrow: *Why is he still in our bed? He's five. Other five-year-olds sleep in their own beds. What did we do wrong? What am I doing wrong?*

She extracted herself carefully—melting off the mattress like goo, one limb at a time, lowering herself to the floor in slow motion so the bed wouldn't shift and wake him—and padded to the bathroom. The house was dark. The dogs hadn't stirred yet. She had maybe an hour before the chaos began—one hour of quiet, of coffee, of trying to write or meditate or simply exist without someone needing something from her.

She made it forty-three minutes.

Sage appeared in the kitchen at 5:30, which was wrong. Sage didn't wake until 6:45 on school days, 11 a.m. on weekends. Sage being awake at 5:30 meant something was wrong.

"Mom." Her daughter's voice was tight. "Look at my face."

Maeve looked. Sage's chin had three new pimples—red, angry, impossible to ignore if you were fourteen and convinced the entire world was staring at your skin.

"Is it worse?" Sage demanded. "It's worse, isn't it?"

First arrow: daughter in pain.

Second arrow: *Here we go. There's no right answer. There's never a right answer.*

"It looks a little better, actually," Maeve tried.

Sage's face crumpled. "You're lying. You always say that. If it was actually better, you'd sound surprised. You sound like you're trying to make me feel better, which means it's bad."

"I'm not—"

"Just tell me the truth for once!"

"I am telling you the truth. It looks—"

"Yesterday you said it was getting better. Now it's 'a little better.' So it's worse. It's getting worse and you won't just say it."

"That's not what I—"

"Forget it." Sage turned away. "I knew I shouldn't have eaten that pizza at Maya's. There was cheese on it. I'm so stupid."

"You're not stupid. One piece of pizza didn't—"

"You don't know that. You don't know anything about acne. You never had it."

This was true. Maeve had been blessed with clear skin as a teenager, a fact that now felt like a betrayal of her daughter. She had no experiential authority here. She could only watch Sage spiral and know that nothing she said would land right.

"What can I do?" Maeve asked. "How can I help?"

"You can't." Sage was already retreating to the bathroom, already reaching for the mirror, already beginning the ritual of examination that would consume the next twenty minutes. "Just—don't buy anything with dairy. I'm serious. Not even bread."

"Bread has dairy?"

"Some bread. Most bread. I don't know. Just check the labels."

The bathroom door closed. Maeve stood in the kitchen, coffee cooling in her hands.

Second arrow: *I should know more about this. I should have researched dairy and acne. I should be a better resource for her. What kind of mother doesn't know that bread has dairy?*

Second arrow: *She's so hard on herself. She gets that from me. I did this to her.*

Second arrow: *I should have had clearer skin to pass on. I should have given her better genes.*

Arrow. Arrow. Arrow.

Eli appeared at 6:15, still in his pajamas, hair flat on one side and vertical on the other. He moved through the kitchen like a ghost, poured himself cereal, and sat at the table with a book already open.

"Morning," Maeve said.

"Morning."

"Sleep okay?"

"Yeah." He didn't look up.

First arrow: the distance. The way he didn't need her anymore, or seemed not to. The way eleven had become a wall she couldn't climb.

But then—

"Mom?" He was looking at her now. "Can you lie with me tonight? When I go to sleep?"

Her heart seized. This was what she wanted, wasn't it? Connection. Access. The bridge between them that she'd been mourning.

"Of course," she said. "I'd love that."

He nodded, returned to his book. Conversation over.

And already—already—she could feel the second arrows forming.

Will I actually love it? Or will I lie there counting seconds, waiting for his breath to slow, calculating how much time until I can leave? What kind of mother doesn't want to lie with her child? What kind of mother has to perform presence instead of feeling it?

She thought about last week. The last time he'd asked. She'd said yes then too—had lain beside him in the dark, his small body warm against hers, his breath gradually slowing. And the whole time, the whole time, she'd been counting. Watching the minutes. Waiting for the twitch of his limbs that meant he'd crossed into sleep. Waiting for permission to leave.

She hadn't felt peace. She'd felt trapped.

And afterward, alone in the hallway, she'd shot herself with so many arrows she'd lost count.

What's wrong with you? He's eleven. He still wants you. Do you know how many mothers would kill for this? And you're lying there counting seconds like it's a prison sentence. You're broken. You're defective. You don't deserve him.

She pushed the memory down. Tonight would be different. Tonight she would be present.

She didn't believe it, but she told herself anyway.

By 6:45, the house had reached full chaos.

Finn was awake, which meant the volume had tripled. He wanted pancakes. Maeve had started pulling out the mix when Sage's voice came from the bathroom, sharp and accusatory.

"DAIRY!!!"

"What about bagels?"

"BAGLES HAVE DAIRY!" Sage screamed from the bathroom.

"Bagels doesn't have—" Maeve checked the bread bag. Third ingredient: milk powder. "Okay, this bagel does. But Sage, the boys can still have pancakes."

"Fine. Make pancakes. I'll just sit here and starve."

"You said you weren't hungry."

"I'M NOT. But it's the principle!"

Finn looked up. "I don't want pancakes anymore."

"Me neither," Eli said, turning a page.

Maeve closed her eyes. Counted to three. Opened them.

"I'll go to the store today. I'll get dairy-free bread and bagels."

"And dairy-free butter," Sage added, finally emerging from the bathroom, face covered in three different spot treatments, each a different shade of medicinal beige. "And check if the peanut butter has dairy."

"Peanut butter doesn't have dairy."

"Some does. Just check."

First arrow: no one will eat anything she knows how to cook.

Second arrows (rapid fire): *Finn hasn't eaten. He's going to starve. How is he even alive? I've failed at the most basic task of motherhood—feeding my child. Other mothers have children who eat. What's wrong with mine? What's wrong with me?*

The guinea pigs began screaming from the living room—their particular whistle-shriek that meant they'd heard the refrigerator open. They associated refrigerator sounds with vegetables. They were usually right.

"Can someone feed the guinea pigs?" Maeve called.

"I did it yesterday," Eli said, not looking up from his book.

"I'm not touching them," Sage said. "They hate me."

"They don't hate you. They're guinea pigs. They don't have opinions about—"

"MAMA!" Finn's scream came from the direction of the kitchen. A different kind of scream. A pain scream.

Maeve ran.

Finn was on the floor, legs splayed, face red with the particular fury of a five-year-old who has been wronged by the universe. The puppy—Beans, four months old, chaos incarnate—was attacking his feet, needle teeth sinking into sock-covered toes.

"What happened?"

"I SLIPPED!" Finn howled. "AND NOW HE'S BITING ME!"

The puddle was evident. Beans had peed again, directly in the center of the kitchen floor. Finn had stepped in it, lost his footing, and gone down. Now Beans, interpreting his screams as an invitation to play, was mounting a full assault on his extremities.

"Beans, no. OFF." Maeve grabbed the puppy, who wiggled with joy at the attention. "Finn, are you okay? Are you hurt?"

"MY BUTT HURTS AND MY TOES HURT AND I'M WET!"

"Okay. Okay. Let me—"

"I HATE THAT DOG!"

"You don't hate—"

"I DO! I HATE HIM! HE PEES EVERYWHERE AND HE BITES ME AND I WANT HIM TO GO AWAY!"

Beans, oblivious to the condemnation, licked Maeve's chin.

First arrow: son on the floor, wet with dog pee, crying.

Second arrows: *Why did we get another dog? We already had two. We didn't need three. This was my idea. I wanted him. Now my son is covered in urine and hates the dog and it's my fault.*

Second arrow: *I should have been watching. I should have seen the puddle. I should have taken him out earlier. I should be better at this.*

Second arrow: *Everyone else's mornings probably don't look like this. Other mothers have systems. Other mothers have control.*

"Let's get you changed," Maeve said, keeping her voice steady through sheer force of will. "Eli, can you clean up the—"

"I'm eating."

"Sage?"

"I'm doing my face."

"Someone needs to clean up the pee."

Silence. The guinea pigs continued screaming. Beans squirmed in her arms. Finn sobbed on the floor.

Maeve put down the puppy, grabbed paper towels, and cleaned it herself.

At 7:15, she couldn't find her keys.

This was the final straw. Not the acne, not the eggs, not the pee, not the screaming guinea pigs or the biting puppy or the five-year-old who refused all food or the eleven-year-old who wanted her presence but not her conversation or the fourteen-year-old who needed her to be an expert in something she knew nothing about.

The keys.

The keys broke her.

"Has anyone seen my keys?" She was opening drawers, checking counters, lifting papers. "They were right here. They're always right here."

"Where did you have them last?" James asked. He'd appeared from the bedroom, showered, dressed, ready for work. Clean. Calm. Untouched by the chaos.

"If I knew where I had them last, I would have them now."

"I'm just trying to help."

"Well, you're not."

The words came out sharp. Sharper than she'd meant. James's face flickered—hurt, frustration, the same expression he'd had last night when she'd snapped about Finn.

First arrow: lost keys.

Second arrow: *I'm a terrible wife. He was just trying to help and I bit his head off. This is why we're not okay. This is why he asked if we were okay. Because I do this. Because I'm like this.*

Second arrow: *I can't find anything. I can't keep track of anything. My brain doesn't work. Other people don't lose their keys. Other people have systems.*

Second arrow: *I'm going to be late for class. I'm going to stand in front of twenty-six people and teach them about not shooting themselves with second arrows and I'm going to be a fraud because I can't even find my keys without having a breakdown.*

"Mom." Eli's voice, quiet. "They're in the bathroom. By the sink."

Maeve stopped. "What?"

"Your keys. I saw them earlier. In the bathroom."

She went. They were there. Right there, next to the soap dispenser, where she must have set them down when she'd gone in to console Sage about her skin.

First arrow: keys were in the bathroom.

That was it. That was the whole thing. Keys in an unexpected location. Not a crisis. Not a catastrophe. Just keys, in a bathroom, waiting to be found.

But the second arrows—god, the second arrows. She'd shot herself a dozen times in the thirty seconds of searching. Failure, incompetence, bad wife, bad mother, fraud, mess. Arrow after arrow after arrow, each one landing in soft tissue, each one drawing blood.

She stood in the bathroom, keys in hand, and caught her own reflection in the mirror.

This, she thought. *This is what I teach about. And I can't even do it.*

. . .

* * *

"GET IN THE CAR. NOW."

It was 7:35. School started at 8:00. The studio was twenty-five minutes away, and class started at 9:00, which meant she had to drop them, drive across town, park, and get into the room with time to set up. The math wasn't working. The math was never working.

"I can't find my shoe," Finn said.

"It's RIGHT THERE. Right there by the door. Where it always is. GET YOUR SHOE AND GET IN THE CAR."

"You don't have to yell." Sage's voice was cold. Superior. The voice of someone cataloguing evidence.

Second arrow: *She's right. You don't have to yell. You're being a terrible mother right now. They're going to remember this. They're going to be in therapy talking about how their mother screamed at them every morning.*

"I'm not yelling," Maeve said, yelling. "I'm just—we're late. We're always late. Can we please, just once, get out the door without—"

"My backpack is too heavy," Eli said. "I think I packed too many books."

"Then take some out."

"But I need them."

"THEN DON'T COMPLAIN ABOUT IT BEING HEAVY."

She heard herself. Heard the sharpness, the edge, the

way her voice had become a weapon. All three children flinched. Even James, still holding his coffee, watching from the kitchen, looked away.

Second arrow: *This is who you are. Not the yoga teacher. Not the calm presence in the heated room. This. This screaming woman who can't get three children out the door without losing her mind. This is the real you.*

They got in the car. Sage in front, arms crossed, staring out the window. Eli in the back, buried in his book, pretending he wasn't there. Finn in his car seat, quietly crying in a way that was worse than screaming—the resigned tears of a child who had learned that sometimes his mother was not safe.

Maeve backed out of the driveway. Her hands were shaking.

First arrow: they were late.

But the second arrows—she'd shot so many at this point that she was more wound than woman. Every harsh word replaying. Every flinch. The look on Finn's face. The ice in Sage's posture. Eli's disappearance.

She drove in silence for three blocks. The guilt built with every block, pressure in her chest, a physical weight.

And then—because this was what she did, because this was the only repair she knew how to offer, because buying things felt like love when she couldn't find any other way to show it:

"Do you guys want Starbucks?"

The car shifted. Sage turned her head slightly. Eli looked up from his book. Even Finn's sniffles paused.

"Really?" Sage asked, suspicion in her voice.

"Really. My treat. Whatever you want."

Second arrow: *You're bribing them. You're trying to buy your way out of being a terrible mother. This is pathetic. This is what bad parents do.*

She ignored the arrow. Kept driving.

"Can I get the pink drink?" Sage asked.

"Yes."

"The large one?"

"The venti. Yes."

"With vanilla cold foam?"

"Whatever you want."

Eli was quiet for a moment. Then: "Can I get a caramel frappuccino?"

"Yes."

"With extra caramel?"

"Yes."

From the back seat, Finn's small voice: "Can I get a cake pop?"

Maeve's hands tightened on the wheel. The cake pop. Of course. The pink cake pop that he'd been obsessed with for three years. The one he'd eat for breakfast, lunch, and dinner if she let him. The one that had to be pink—not chocolate, not birthday cake, only pink—and had to come from the Starbucks on Main Street—not the one by the freeway, not the one in the shopping center, only the one on Main Street—because somehow, impossibly, he could tell the difference."

"We have to go to the Main Street Starbucks," she

said, already calculating. It was out of the way. It would make them later. "Is that okay with everyone?"

"Why that one?" Sage asked.

"Because Finn's cake pops only come from there."

Sage rolled her eyes but didn't argue. The bribe was working. The repair was in process.

They pulled into the drive-through at 7:52. The line had four cars.

Second arrow: *You don't have time for this. You're going to be late to class. You're going to walk in frazzled and sweaty and fake and everyone will know. Everyone will see through you.*

She stayed in line.

"What do you want, Mom?" Eli asked. His voice was soft now. The sharp edges of the morning already smoothing.

"I'm okay."

"You should get something."

"Really, I'm—"

"Get your coffee," Sage said. Still cold, but something underneath it. Something that might have been forgiveness making its way to the surface. "You always get that iced Americano thing."

"With heavy cream," Finn added from the back. "Mama gets heavy cream."

Maeve's throat tightened. They knew her order. They paid attention. Even through the chaos, even through the screaming and the snapping and the lost keys—they saw her. They knew what she liked.

"Okay," she said. "I'll get my coffee."

She ordered. Sage's pink drink, venti, with vanilla cold foam—seven dollars. Eli's caramel frappuccino with extra caramel—six dollars. Finn's pink cake pop—three fifty. Her own Americano with heavy cream—five dollars. And then Finn wanted a bagel too—but only if it didn't have dairy (she asked; it didn't)—and Sage decided she wanted a cheese danish and then immediately un-ordered it because cheese was dairy (was it? Maeve didn't know), and Eli wanted a bacon sandwich, and by the time they pulled away from the window, the total was forty-three dollars.

Forty-three dollars to apologize for yelling at her children.

Second arrow: *You can't afford this. The tuition is due next week. You just spent forty-three dollars on guilt coffee and cake pops because you couldn't keep your temper for one morning.*

Second arrow: *And it won't even work. They'll forgive you, and tomorrow you'll do the same thing. You'll yell again. You'll snap again. And you'll buy them Starbucks again. This is the cycle. This is who you are.*

She handed back drinks and food. Watched Finn bite into his pink cake pop with the singular focus of a child who has finally received what he wanted. Watched Sage sip her pink drink, the anger slowly melting. Watched Eli eat his sandwich and return to his book, peace restored.

First arrow: she had been late, stressed, unkind.

Second arrow: she had tried to repair with money.

Third arrow, fourth, fifth—an endless volley of self-recrimination that continued even as the children softened, even as the morning smoothed, even as the crisis passed.

She dropped them at school at 8:07. Seven minutes late. Each child climbed out with their Starbucks, their backpacks, their various moods.

"Have a good day," Maeve said. "I love you."

"Love you too." Eli, already walking.

"Bye." Sage, over her shoulder, still cool but warming.

"LOVE YOU MAMA!" Finn, screaming across the parking lot at full volume, cake pop in hand, completely recovered from the trauma of an hour ago.

Maeve watched them go. Three children, three grades, three separate lives she was somehow supposed to track and support and show up for.

She checked the clock. 8:09. Class started at 9:00. Twenty-five minutes to the studio, plus parking so add ten, plus setup.

She might make it. Barely.

Second arrow: *This is not sustainable. Something has to change. You cannot keep doing this.*

She started driving.

* * *

. . .

She walked into the studio at 8:50.

Ten minutes. She had ten minutes to set up the room, change her energy, transform from the screaming mother in the car to the calm teacher on the mat.

She did it. She always did it. The compartmentalization was its own kind of violence—shoving everything down, plastering on serenity, pretending the last two hours hadn't happened.

The students filed in. Arranged themselves on their mats. Closed their eyes.

Maeve stood at the front of the room and talked about arrows.

"The first arrow is pain," she said, her voice steady, her heart still racing. "It's unavoidable. It lands. We feel it. But the second arrow—the second arrow is the story we tell about the pain. The judgment we add. The suffering we create on top of the hurt."

She believed every word. She also knew she had shot herself with approximately forty-seven arrows that morning, and the wounds were still bleeding.

"The practice isn't about never getting hit by the first arrow," she continued. "It's about learning to notice when we pick up the second one. Learning to feel the pain without adding to it. Learning to say, 'this hurts,' without adding, 'and that means something is wrong with me.'"

In the front row, the Tuesday regular nodded. The woman who had shot herself with many arrows.

They were all that woman, Maeve thought. Every

single person in this room. Every single person walking around with wounds from arrows they'd fired at themselves.

"Find your first pose," she said. "Butterfly. Let's begin."

The class unfolded. The students folded. The heat built. The silence deepened.

Maeve walked the room, adjusting, offering props, speaking the words she knew by heart.

"Notice the second arrow."

"Can you feel the sensation without the story?"

"What if you didn't add anything to this moment?"

In Dragonfly, a woman began to cry. Quietly, the way people cried in yin—not sobbing, just leaking. Tears sliding down cheeks, dripping onto mats.

Maeve knelt beside her.

"You're okay," she whispered. "Let it move through."

The woman nodded, eyes closed.

Maeve moved on. But something had shifted in her chest. Watching this woman feel her feelings without trying to fix them—it cracked something open.

Let it move through.

Wasn't that what she needed? Not to stop shooting arrows—that was too much to ask this morning. But to let the wounds breathe. To stop adding pressure to the places that were already bleeding.

She returned to the front of the room.

"Last few breaths here," she said. "And I want to offer you something. The second arrow isn't a failure. It's a habit. It's what minds do. They add. They interpret. They create meaning. That's not wrong—it's human."

She paused. This wasn't part of her usual script. This was something else. Something truer.

"The practice isn't about being perfect. It's not about never shooting the second arrow. It's about noticing. Just noticing. 'Oh, there I go again. There's the story. There's the judgment. There's the arrow.' And then—gently, kindly—putting it down. Not because you're bad for picking it up. But because you don't have to keep holding it."

She thought about Finn, screaming on the floor. About Sage, examining her face in the mirror. About Eli, asking for her presence and receiving her performance. About James, trying to help and being snapped at. About forty-three dollars at Starbucks and the drive-through line that made her later and the guilt that made her go anyway.

Arrows. All of it, arrows.

But here was the thing: she was still standing. Still teaching. Still showing up.

The first arrows had landed. The morning had happened. It wasn't pretty.

But she was here.

* * *

. . .

After class, a student lingered.

It was the Tuesday regular. The nodding woman. She stood by the door, mat rolled under her arm, hesitating.

"That was..." She paused. Started again. "That was really helpful today. The thing you said at the end. About the second arrow not being a failure."

Maeve nodded. "I'm glad it landed."

"I've been shooting myself with so many arrows lately." The woman's voice cracked slightly. "My mom is sick. And I keep—I keep making it mean something about me. Like I should be handling it better. Like other people would be stronger."

First arrow: her mom is sick.

Second arrow: I should be handling it better.

Maeve recognized the pattern. She lived inside it.

"That's so hard," she said. "I'm sorry about your mom."

"Thanks." The woman wiped her eyes. "Anyway. I just wanted to say—I needed to hear that today. The part about being human. About it being a habit, not a failure."

"I needed to say it," Maeve admitted. "I had a rough morning."

The woman looked surprised. As if yoga teachers didn't have rough mornings. As if serenity was a permanent state rather than a temporary pose.

"Really?"

"Really. Lost my keys. Yelled at my kids. Spent forty dollars at Starbucks trying to apologize."

The woman laughed—a real laugh, surprised and

warm. "That sounds like my morning. Minus the Starbucks. I should try the Starbucks thing."

"It doesn't actually help," Maeve said. "But it feels like it might."

"Sometimes that's enough."

They stood there for a moment, two women who had shot themselves with many arrows, finding something shared in the admission.

"See you next week?" the woman asked.

"I'll be here."

The woman left. Maeve stood alone in the empty room, the heat still lingering, the mats still arranged in their careful rows.

She thought about the morning. The chaos, the snapping, the guilt, the repair. The forty-three dollars she couldn't really afford. The pink cake pop that had to come from one specific Starbucks. The way Finn had screamed "LOVE YOU MAMA" across the parking lot like nothing bad had ever happened.

First arrow: the morning was hard.

Second arrow: I'm a bad mother.

Third arrow: I'm a fraud.

Fourth arrow: I can't do this.

She felt them all, stuck in her ribs, throbbing.

And then—gently, carefully—she began to pull them out.

Not because the morning hadn't happened. It had. Not because she'd handled it well. She hadn't. Not because the guilt wasn't real or the snapping wasn't harmful or the money wasn't a problem.

But because she couldn't keep holding them. Because the weight was too much. Because the bleeding had to stop somewhere.

Oh, she thought, *there I go again. There's the story. There's the judgment. There's the arrow.*

She put it down.

Not perfectly. Not completely. But a little. Just a little.

And that, she decided, would have to be enough for today.

* * *

That night, she lay with Eli.

His room was dark except for the glow of a nightlight—a moon, pale blue, that he'd had since he was small. He was too old for it now, probably. But he hadn't asked her to remove it, and she hadn't offered.

She lay on top of the covers beside him, her body stiff, her mind already counting.

He's not asleep yet. How long has it been? Two minutes? Five? Why isn't he asleep yet? I have dishes to do. I have emails to answer. I have—

Second arrow. She caught it mid-flight.

Oh. There it is. The counting. The escape planning. The story about how I should be somewhere else.

She put it down.

Tried, anyway.

Eli shifted beside her. His breathing was slow but not yet heavy. Not yet the twitch of limbs that meant sleep.

"Mom?"

"Yeah?"

"Thanks for lying with me."

"Of course, baby."

"I know you're busy."

The words landed like a blow. *I know you're busy.* The story of their relationship. The excuse she gave, the understanding he offered. Busy. Always busy. Too busy to lie with him without counting. Too busy to see him without being reminded.

"I'm not too busy for you," she said. And meant it. And wasn't sure she'd ever proven it.

"Okay." He was quiet for a moment. Then: "Mom?"

"Yeah?"

"I don't actually need you to stay until I fall asleep. I just like when you're here for a little bit."

She turned her head to look at him. In the blue glow of the moon nightlight, he looked younger than eleven. He looked like the boy he'd been at six, at four, at two—small and certain and hers.

"I like being here too," she said.

And this time, she meant it differently. Not as performance. Not as obligation. But as truth—incomplete, imperfect, but true.

She stayed ten more minutes. Felt his body relax beside her. Listened to his breathing slow. And when she finally left—quietly, carefully—she didn't feel like she was escaping.

She felt like she was leaving something good.

James was awake when she climbed into bed.

"How was it?" he asked. "Lying with Eli?"

"Good," she said. "It was actually good."

He reached for her hand in the dark. She let him take it.

"I'm sorry about this morning," she said. "About snapping at you."

"I know."

"I was stressed."

"I know."

"That's not an excuse."

"I know that too."

They lay there, hands linked, the silence comfortable in a way it hadn't been in a while.

"I shot myself with a lot of arrows today," Maeve said. "That was the lesson. In class. The second arrow."

"Tell me."

So she did. The whole morning—the acne, the eggs, the pee, the keys, the yelling, the Starbucks. The forty-three dollars. The pink cake pop from the right Starbucks. The way she'd walked into class four minutes before it started and somehow found the words anyway.

James listened. He was good at listening. It was one of the things she forgot about him, in the chaos of days—how he could hold space without trying to fix.

"That's a lot of arrows," he said, when she finished.

"Yeah."

"You know most of them weren't real, right? Like—the 'bad mother' one. That's not real."

"It felt real."

"Feelings aren't facts."

She almost laughed. "Did you just quote a yoga teacher at me?"

"I've been listening for fifteen years. Some of it stuck."

She squeezed his hand. "We should talk. The thing you asked about—whether we're okay."

"We don't have to do it tonight."

"I know. But soon."

"Soon," he agreed.

Finn's door opened down the hall. Small footsteps padded toward their room. A moment later, a small body was climbing into the bed between them, arranging himself perpendicular, already rotating toward his first position.

"He's back," James said.

"He's back."

"Should we—"

"No." Maeve sighed. "Not tonight. Tonight he can stay."

First arrow: there was a five-year-old in their bed again.

She waited for the second arrow. The story about how this was wrong, how other parents had boundaries, how she was failing by allowing it.

The arrow formed. Rose. Began its flight.

And then—somehow—she let it fall.

Tonight he can stay. Tonight this is enough. Tonight I don't have to fix anything.

Finn's feet found her ribs. His small body radiated heat like a furnace.

First arrow only.

She closed her eyes.

She slept.

3

Transparent and Kind
You can say almost anything to anyone if you say it with honesty and love.

There was a sign on the studio door.

Maeve had made it herself, printed it on cardstock, laminated it at the office supply store. It said: *This is a meditation space. Please enter quietly and allow others to prepare for practice in silence.*

No one ever read it.

She watched them walk past it every single class—chatting, laughing, phones still in hand, conversations continuing from the parking lot through the lobby and onto their mats. The sign might as well have been invisible. A decoration. A suggestion that everyone had collectively agreed to ignore.

Today she was going to say something.

She stood at the front of the room, Thursday morning, waiting for the last few students to settle. The room was warm, the heaters humming, the smell of eucalyptus hanging in the air. Twenty-one mats arranged in careful rows. Twenty-one people who had carved out ninety minutes from their lives to be here.

"Before we begin," Maeve said, "I want to point something out."

The room quieted. A few people looked up, curious.

"There's a sign on the door. You've probably walked past it a hundred times." She smiled, keeping her voice light. "It asks that we enter the studio quietly and allow the space to be a meditation space before class begins."

She paused. Scanned the room. Some nodded. Others looked away—the particular avoidance of people who suspected they might be the reason for this announcement.

"This isn't directed at anyone specifically," Maeve continued. "I'm saying it to everyone because I want us all to hold this space together. The minutes before class—they matter. Some of you have just come from difficult mornings. Traffic. Arguments. Stress. Those few minutes of quiet before we begin? That's part of the practice. That's when you start to transition from out there to in here."

She let that land.

"So. Moving forward. When you enter, find your mat, settle in, close your eyes. Let the room be quiet. Let yourself arrive. And if you need to chat, the lobby is right outside." Another smile. "Okay. Let's begin."

She moved into the opening centering, guiding them through breath awareness, watching the room shift into stillness.

But part of her was still thinking about boundaries. About the sign no one read. About the conversations she'd had to have—and the ones she still needed to.

"Today we're going to talk about something uncomfortable," she said, once they were settled into their first pose—a supported child's pose, foreheads resting on stacked fists or blocks. "We're going to talk about having hard conversations."

She walked the room slowly, her voice low and steady.

"There's a phrase I come back to again and again: transparent and kind. It means you can say almost anything to anyone—if you say it with honesty and love."

She paused beside a student whose shoulders were creeping toward her ears. Placed a gentle hand on her back. The shoulders dropped.

"Transparent means honest. Direct. No weird euphemisms, no beating around the bush. You say the thing that needs to be said."

She moved on, weaving between mats.

"Kind means you're doing it for them, not at them. Your intention is care, not punishment. You're offering information, not judgment. You're private, not public. Warm, not cold."

In the front row, a woman was nodding. The Tuesday regular—though today was Thursday, so maybe she was the Every Day regular now. She'd been coming more often lately. Her mom was still sick.

"Here's the thing," Maeve continued. "Most of us avoid hard conversations. We don't want to be mean. We don't want to make people uncomfortable. So we stay quiet. We tolerate things that aren't working. We let resentment build instead of addressing the issue."

She returned to the front of the room.

"But that's not kindness. That's avoidance. Real kindness is caring enough to have the conversation. Real kindness is trusting the other person to handle the truth."

She let them sit with that.

"Think about your own life," she said. "Is there a conversation you've been avoiding? Something you need to say to someone—but you've been too scared, too polite, too worried about how it will land?"

Silence. The room breathed.

"The practice isn't about having these conversations perfectly. It's about having them at all. Transparent and kind. Honest and loving. Both. Not one or the other."

She guided them into the next pose—a gentle twist, releasing the spine.

"And here's the secret," she added. "Most people, when you tell them something hard with genuine care? They thank you. They say, 'I had no idea. Thank you for telling me.' Because they didn't know. They were in their own world, doing their thing, not realizing how it landed for everyone else."

She thought about her own conversations. The ones she'd had. The ones she still needed to have.

"Today, as we practice, notice where you're holding back. Where you're tolerating something instead of addressing it. Where avoidance is masquerading as kindness."

She paused.

"And ask yourself: what would transparent and kind look like here?"

The class unfolded. They moved through hip openers, heart openers, gentle backbends. Maeve wove the theme throughout—returning to it in quiet moments, letting it settle into the spaces between poses.

"Boundaries are a form of kindness," she said during a long pigeon hold. "When you set a boundary, you're not being mean. You're being clear. You're telling people how to be in relationship with you. That's a gift."

She scanned the room.

"We think boundaries push people away. But actually, they create safety. They let people know where they stand. They build trust."

She pressed on someones hips helping them release deeper.

"The hardest boundaries to set are often with the people we love most. Partners. Children. Family. Friends.

We don't want to hurt them. We don't want to seem selfish. So we give and give until there's nothing left."

She thought about her own morning. About James. About the conversation she'd finally had.

"But here's the truth: you can't pour from an empty cup. And refusing to set boundaries doesn't make you generous. It makes you depleted. And depleted people can't show up fully for anyone."

She guided them toward savasana, the room softening, bodies releasing into the floor.

"As you rest," she said, her voice barely above a whisper, "ask yourself: where do I need to set a boundary? Where am I giving more than I have? Where is my kindness actually avoidance?"

She let the silence hold them.

"And then ask: what would transparent and kind look like there?"

* * *

After class, Linda lingered.

Maeve saw her hovering by the door as the other students filed out—rolling up mats, gathering water bottles, murmuring goodbyes. Linda always lingered. She was a good student, consistent, showed up twice a week without fail. She was also lonely. Maeve could see it in the way she reached for connection, the way conversations that should take two minutes stretched to fifteen, twenty, thirty.

"Maeve, do you have a second?"

Maeve glanced at the clock. She had exactly forty-five minutes before she needed to pick up Finn. Forty-five minutes that she'd planned to use for herself—to sit in the quiet studio, to meditate, to exist without anyone needing anything from her.

"Of course," she said. "What's up?"

"I just wanted to tell you about what's going on with my son."

And Linda was off. Her son—thirty-two, lived in Seattle, worked in tech. His girlfriend, who Linda didn't trust. The apartment they'd just moved into together, which Linda thought was too expensive. The phone call they'd had last night where he'd seemed distant, distracted, not himself.

Maeve listened. She nodded in the right places. She made the appropriate sounds of sympathy and understanding.

But inside, she was doing math.

This has already been four minutes. If it goes another ten, that's fourteen minutes gone. I'll have thirty-one minutes left. Minus the five minutes it takes to lock up, that's twenty-six. Minus the ten-minute drive, that's sixteen. Sixteen minutes to sit. To breathe. To be alone.

She hated herself for counting. Linda was a person, not an interruption. Her loneliness was real. Her need for connection was valid.

But so was Maeve's need for solitude.

Transparent and kind, she thought. *I literally just taught this.*

"—and then she said she didn't think they needed to come for Thanksgiving, which I thought was just—"

"Linda." Maeve touched her arm gently. "I'm so sorry to interrupt. This sounds really hard, and I can tell you're worried about him."

Linda stopped, surprised. "Oh. Yes. I am."

"I want to hear more about it. But I have to be honest with you—I have about forty-five minutes before my next commitment, and I really need some of that time to decompress. It's how I take care of myself so I can keep showing up for classes."

She watched Linda's face. The flicker of hurt. The recalibration.

"Would it be okay if we continued this another time? Maybe we could grab coffee sometime, and you could tell me the whole story properly?"

Linda blinked. Then—to Maeve's relief—she smiled.

"Of course. I'm sorry. I didn't realize—I just start talking and I don't—"

"You don't have to apologize. I love that you share with me. I just needed to be honest about my time today."

"No, no, you're right. I do this. I know I do this." Linda laughed, a little embarrassed. "My daughter tells me the same thing. 'Mom, you've been talking for twenty minutes and you haven't asked me a single question.'"

Maeve smiled. "We all do it. I do it too."

"Well." Linda gathered her things. "Thank you for saying something. I appreciate the honesty."

"Thank you for understanding."

Linda left. Maeve stood alone in the empty studio.

Twenty-eight minutes. She had twenty-eight minutes.

She sat down on her mat, closed her eyes, and breathed.

Transparent and kind. Both. Not one or the other.

She'd done it. It had felt hard. It had felt selfish.

But it was neither. It was just clear.

And now she had twenty-eight minutes of silence. Twenty-eight minutes of nothing but her own breath.

It was enough. It was more than enough.

It was everything.

* * *

The boundary with James had been harder.

It had happened three days ago. 4:15 a.m. Maeve had been awake since 3:47, had slid out of bed like goo—one limb at a time, lowering herself to the floor in slow motion so the mattress wouldn't shift—and had made her way downstairs to the living room. Her sacred time. The only hours that belonged entirely to her.

She'd made coffee. Settled onto the couch. Closed her eyes to meditate.

And then she'd heard it.

Footsteps on the stairs. The particular creak of the third step, the one that always gave James away.

Her stomach dropped.

He appeared in the doorway, wearing only boxers, grinning in that particular way that meant he'd woken up with one thing on his mind.

"Hey," he said, his voice low. "Couldn't sleep. Noticed you were gone."

"I'm meditating," she said.

"I can see that." He moved toward her. "Want some company?"

She knew what he was asking. And part of her—the part that remembered when they'd been young, when they'd had time, when his desire had felt like a gift instead of an intrusion—wanted to say yes.

But the larger part of her, the part that had clawed these morning hours out of nothing, that had fought for this sliver of solitude, that knew she had exactly ninety minutes before the children woke and the chaos began—that part wanted to scream.

She didn't scream. She said yes.

Because that's what she did. Because the guilt of saying no felt worse than the loss of the time. Because James worked hard and deserved to feel wanted and what kind of wife turned down her husband?

They went upstairs. It was quick. He fell back asleep immediately, satisfied, sprawled across the bed.

Maeve lay beside him, staring at the ceiling, doing math.

It's 4:47 now. If I go back downstairs, I'll have maybe

forty-five minutes before Finn wakes up. But I'm not in the meditation space anymore. I'm in my head. I'm resentful. I'm calculating. This isn't presence. This is performance.

She'd lost the morning. Not just the time—the quality of it. The stillness she'd been protecting.

And she'd done it to herself.

The next morning, she'd set the boundary.

It was 4:02 a.m. She was downstairs on the couch, coffee set on the side table, eyes closed, when she heard it—the creak of the floorboards above her. The bathroom door. The flush. Then footsteps moving toward the stairs.

She intercepted him at the bottom.

"Hey," she whispered. "Go back to bed."

"I was going to come down—"

"I know. But I need you not to."

His face did something complicated. Hurt. Confusion. The particular male bewilderment of being rejected.

"I need these hours," she said. "I need them to be mine. Just mine. It's how I survive the day."

"I just wanted to—"

"I know what you wanted." She softened her voice, touched his arm. "And I love that you want me. I do. But this time—the time before the kids wake up—it's the only time I have. And when you come downstairs, even with good intentions, it takes something from me."

He was quiet for a moment.

"You could have just said no last time."

"I know. I should have. I didn't because I felt guilty. But the guilt made me resentful, and the resentment made me lose the whole morning anyway. So now I'm saying it in advance. This time is mine. Find me later. Find another window. But not this one."

James stood in the doorway, processing. She could see him deciding how to feel—whether to be hurt, whether to argue, whether to accept.

Finally, he nodded.

"Okay."

"Okay?"

"Yeah. Okay. I hear you." He paused. "I'm sorry. I didn't realize it meant that much to you."

"It means everything."

He leaned in, kissed her forehead. "I'll go back to bed."

"Thank you."

He went. She stood in the hallway for a moment, heart pounding, guilt swirling.

Was that too harsh? Should I have been softer? He just wanted to connect. What kind of wife—

She stopped the spiral.

Transparent and kind. Transparent and kind.

She'd been both. She'd told the truth. She'd done it with love. The rest was not her responsibility.

She went downstairs. Made her coffee. Sat on the couch.

And for the first time in weeks, she actually meditated.

* * *

She meditated blissfully, journaled, and enjoyed the peace for approximately an hour.

Then Sage had appeared at 5:04, face puffy, eyes red.

"I can't sleep. My face is so bad. Look at it."

Then Finn at 5:23, crying about a nightmare, climbing into her lap on the couch, destroying any hope of continued solitude.

Then Eli at 6:15, quiet as always, but needing breakfast, needing attention, needing her to remember he existed.

By 7:30, she was running late. The kitchen was chaos. Beans had peed twice. The guinea pigs were screaming. Sage was having a breakdown about a shirt that had apparently shrunk in the wash. Eli couldn't find his library book. Finn was refusing all food except the pink cake pop they didn't have.

"GET IN THE CAR."

She heard herself yelling again. Heard the sharp edge in her voice.

Second arrow: You're doing it again. You're always doing

it. The boundary with James didn't fix anything. You're still a mess. You're still failing.

She pushed the arrow down. No time for self-recrimination. No time for anything.

They made it to school by 8:09. Nine minutes late. Each child tumbled out of the car with their backpacks and their various grievances.

"Love you," Maeve called.

"Bye," from Sage, still cold about the shirt.

"Love you too," from Eli, already walking.

"LOVE YOU MAMA!" from Finn, recovered entirely, waving wildly as he ran toward the kindergarten door.

Maeve watched them go.

Then she looked down at herself.

Mismatched patterns. A striped shirt with floral leggings. She'd grabbed them from the clean clothes bin—the one that was overflowing because she never had time to put laundry away—on her way out the door. Her hair was in a messy bun that had started as a topknot and devolved into something closer to a bird's nest. She hadn't looked in a mirror. She hadn't brushed her teeth.

She was going to stand in front of twenty-one people and teach about boundaries.

She looked like she had none.

First arrow: this is how you look today.

She waited for the second arrow. The judgment, the shame, the story about what this meant about her as a person, a mother, a teacher.

Oh, she thought. *There it is. There's the hand reaching for the arrow.*

She didn't pick it up.
She just drove to the studio.

* * *

That night, she sat with Sage.

Not the usual bedtime visit—this was earlier, 8 p.m., before the boys were asleep. Sage had been crying about her skin again, had spent twenty minutes in front of the mirror cataloguing every flaw.

Maeve knocked. Waited.

"What."

"Can I come in?"

Silence. Then: "Fine."

Maeve entered. Sage was on her bed, phone in hand, face blotchy from crying.

"I want to talk to you about something," Maeve said.

"If it's about my face, I don't want to hear it."

"It's not about your face." Maeve sat on the edge of the bed. "It's about this morning. The way I yelled at everyone."

Sage looked up, surprised.

"I'm sorry," Maeve said. "I was stressed and overwhelmed and I took it out on you guys. That wasn't fair."

Sage was quiet for a moment. Then: "It's fine. You're always stressed."

The words landed like a slap.

You're always stressed.

Was that how her daughter saw her? Not as a teacher of peace and presence, but as a stressed-out woman who yelled in the mornings and apologized at night?

"I am stressed a lot," Maeve admitted. "More than I should be. I'm working on it."

"How?"

"Boundaries. Setting better boundaries. Asking for what I need instead of just giving until I'm empty."

Sage considered this. "Like what?"

"Like... this morning, I needed time to myself before you guys woke up. I had it, for a little while. But then everything went sideways and I lost it, and by the time we were leaving, I had nothing left. So I yelled."

"That doesn't sound like a boundary. That sounds like a failure."

Maeve almost laughed. "You're right. It was a failure. The boundary is what I'm trying to build. The failing is what happens while I'm learning."

Sage was quiet for a moment. Then, unexpectedly: "I need boundaries too."

"Yeah?"

"Like with you. And the acne thing."

Maeve's chest tightened. "Tell me."

"I need you to stop answering when I ask if it looks better or worse."

Maeve blinked. "But you ask me. Every day. Sometimes twice a day."

"I know. And I need you to stop answering. Because there's no right answer. If you say it's better, I think you're lying. If you say it's worse, I spiral. If you say it's the same, I think you're not really looking. I'm putting you in an impossible situation and then getting mad at you for whatever you say."

Maeve stared at her daughter. This was—this was remarkably self-aware for fourteen.

"So what do you want me to say? When you ask?"

Sage thought about it. "Maybe just... 'I'm not going to answer that.' And then change the subject. Or hug me. Or tell me I'm being crazy. I don't know. Just don't play the game with me."

First arrow: her daughter was asking for help setting a boundary with herself.

Maeve waited for the second arrow—the one about how she should have figured this out sooner, should have known not to engage, should have been a better mother.

She let it fall.

"Okay," she said. "I can do that. When you ask, I'll say 'I'm not playing this game' and then I'll hug you instead."

"That might be annoying."

"Probably. But it's better than the alternative."

Sage almost smiled. "Yeah. Probably."

"That's okay. Just... try."

"I'll try."

Sage looked at her for a long moment. Something shifted in her face—the armor softening, the teenager receding, the child underneath briefly visible.

"Thanks, Mom."

"Thank you for telling me. That was brave."

Sage shrugged, but Maeve could see she was pleased. "Transparent and kind, right? Isn't that what you always say?"

Maeve blinked. "You listen to my classes?"

"Sometimes. When I can't sleep. I watch the recordings on YouTube."

Maeve's throat tightened. This girl. This impossible, beautiful, maddening girl. Watching her mother's yoga videos in secret, absorbing teachings she'd never admit to caring about.

"I didn't know that."

"Yeah, well." Sage looked away. "Don't make it weird."

"I won't."

They sat in silence for a moment. Then Sage said: "Mom?"

"Yeah?"

"Your outfit today was really bad. Like, really bad."

Maeve laughed—a real laugh, surprised out of her. "I know. I grabbed it from the laundry bin."

"The stripes with the flowers? It was a lot."

"I didn't have time to look in a mirror."

"Clearly."

But Sage was smiling now. A real smile, the first one Maeve had seen all day.

"I'll try to do better tomorrow," Maeve said.

"Don't make promises you can't keep."

"Fair enough."

She stood to leave. At the door, she turned back.

"Sage?"

"Yeah?"

"I'm not going to say anything about your face. But I am going to say this: you're beautiful. Not despite anything. Just... you're beautiful. Okay?"

Sage rolled her eyes. "You have to say that. You're my mom."

"I have to say it. But I also mean it."

She left before Sage could respond. But she heard it anyway—the small sound her daughter made, somewhere between dismissal and gratitude.

It was enough.

* * *

James was awake when she came to bed.

"How was your day?" he asked.

"Long. Hard. Good."

"Good hard or bad hard?"

"Both." She climbed under the covers, let him pull her close. "I set some boundaries today."

"Yeah?"

"Yeah. With a student who talks too much after class. With Sage about her skin. With myself about... everything."

"How did it go?"

"Terrifying. But okay. I think people actually respected it. Or at least they pretended to."

James was quiet for a moment. Then: "Thank you. For the boundary you set with me."

She turned to look at him. "Really?"

"Yeah. I didn't like it at first. It felt like rejection. But then I thought about it, and... you were right. I was taking something that wasn't mine to take. Those hours in the morning—they're yours. I was crashing into them because it was convenient for me, not because you wanted me there."

"I do want you. Just... not then."

"I know. I get it now." He kissed her forehead. "Find me later, you said. So I'm finding you now. Is this okay?"

She considered. The day had been long. She was tired. Part of her wanted to just sleep.

But this was different. This was the window she'd asked for. This was him respecting the boundary and finding another way.

"This is okay," she said.

"Yeah?"

"Yeah."

He pulled her closer.

And for once, it didn't feel like a theft. It felt like a gift.

Later, in the dark, Finn's door opened.

Small footsteps. The creak of the mattress. A small body arranging itself perpendicular between them.

"He's back," James murmured.

"He's back."

"Should we—"

"No." Maeve sighed. "Not tonight. We'll work on that boundary another day."

"Fair enough."

Finn's feet found her ribs. His small body radiated heat.

She thought about all the boundaries she'd set today. The sign on the door. The conversation with Linda. The talk with Sage. The ongoing negotiation with James.

And this one—the five-year-old in their bed—still unaddressed. Still too hard.

You can't do everything at once, she told herself. *You can only do the next thing.*

Today she'd done several next things. Tomorrow there would be more.

For now, this was enough.

Finn's breathing slowed. James's arm tightened around her.

Transparent and kind, she thought. *With others. With yourself. Both.*

She was learning.

Slowly, imperfectly, but learning.

She closed her eyes.

She slept.

4

The Empty Boat

If the boat is empty, there's no one to be angry at.

There's a Zen story about a man in a boat.

Maeve stood at the front of the room, Sunday morning, 8 a.m., the early class that drew the dedicated ones—the people who chose yoga over sleeping in, who wanted to start their week with intention. Eighteen students today. A smaller room, more intimate.

"He's out on a lake," she said, "rowing peacefully, enjoying the quiet, when suddenly another boat crashes into his. He's furious. He turns around, ready to yell at whoever just ruined his peaceful morning—"

She paused.

"And the boat is empty. It had drifted loose from

somewhere upstream. There's no one in it. No one to blame. No one to be angry at."

She let that sit.

"Here's what's interesting. When the man saw the empty boat, his anger vanished. Immediately. Because there was no one to direct it at. No story to tell about someone being careless or rude or intentionally crashing into him. Just an empty boat. Just a thing that happened."

She walked slowly through the room, weaving between mats.

"But what if someone had been in the boat? Same crash. Same disruption. Same spilled coffee, same jolt to his morning. But now there's a person to blame. Now there's a story: they weren't paying attention, they don't care about anyone else, what kind of idiot doesn't watch where they're going?"

She returned to the front.

"The crash is the same either way. But our suffering —that comes from the story. That comes from believing someone did this to us on purpose. That comes from filling the empty boat with a villain."

A woman in the front row was nodding. The Tuesday-and-Sunday regular.

"Today," Maeve said, "I want you to notice where you're filling empty boats. Where you're creating stories about other people's intentions. Where you're assuming malice when there might just be... an empty boat. A person drifting through their own life, crashing into yours by accident, not design."

She guided them into child's pose, foreheads resting on the mat.

"This doesn't mean we don't have boundaries. This doesn't mean we accept bad behavior. But it does mean we can hold people accountable without making up stories about who they are and why they did what they did."

She paused.

"We can address the crash without filling the boat with a monster."

The class moved through a slow, grounding flow. Standing poses, hip openers, gentle twists. Maeve wove the theme throughout.

"Notice when you start creating a story," she said during warrior two. "About the person next to you, about yourself, about me. We're all just boats, drifting, occasionally crashing. Most of it isn't personal."

She thought about boats. About stories. About the man she'd been married to for years, who still sometimes felt like a stranger. About the conversation they kept postponing. About the stories she was telling herself—that he didn't understand her, that he couldn't meet her where she was, that the distance between them meant something was fundamentally broken.

Were those stories true? Or was she filling an empty boat?

She didn't know. She wasn't sure she wanted to find out.

. . .

* * *

The boys had shown up three weeks ago.

Neighborhood kids—ten, eleven years old. That awkward age where childhood was receding but adolescence hadn't fully arrived. They rode bikes in loose packs, congregated on corners, made noise that wasn't quite trouble but wasn't quite innocent either.

Eli had started hanging out with them. Coming home later than usual, vague about where he'd been. "Just around," he'd say. "With some guys."

Maeve had been cautiously optimistic. Eli needed friends. He spent so much time alone, buried in books, invisible in his own house. If he was finding a group, finding his people, that was good. That was healthy.

One afternoon, two of the boys had ended up in her kitchen.

She'd been making snacks when they appeared—following Eli through the back door, hovering awkwardly by the counter. One was tall and gangly, all elbows and Adam's apple. The other was shorter, stockier, with a face that hadn't quite decided what it would become.

"Mom, this is Tyler and Jack," Eli said. "Can they have some food?"

"Of course." Maeve pulled out chips, salsa, the leftover pizza from last night. "Help yourselves."

The boys descended on the food like they hadn't eaten in days. Maeve watched them, charmed despite herself. They were so young. So hungry. So transparently desperate to seem cool while also clearly just being kids.

"So how do you guys know Eli?" she asked.

"School," Tyler said, mouth full of chips.

"We're in the same PE class," Jack added. "Eli's pretty fast."

Eli ducked his head, embarrassed and pleased.

They stayed for an hour. Talked about video games, about a teacher they all hated, about some drama involving a girl named Madison who had allegedly said something about someone's sister. Normal kid stuff. Maeve listened, asked questions, laughed at their jokes.

After they left, she felt good. Eli had friends. Real friends who came to the house and ate her food and treated him like one of them.

Then the text came.

It was from Deborah, three houses down. The one who sat on the HOA board and knew everything about everyone.

Hey—saw those boys at your place. Just FYI, the one called Tyler isn't supposed to be in the community. The board sent a letter to his parents after the incident with the Hendersons' mailbox. Just thought you should know.

Maeve stared at the text.

The incident with the Hendersons' mailbox. She vaguely remembered hearing about it—something about vandalism, about property damage, about "those boys" being a problem. She'd filed it away as neighborhood gossip, the kind of thing that got exaggerated in the retelling.

She typed back: *Thanks for letting me know.*

Then she put down the phone and didn't think about it again.

Because what was she supposed to do? Ban a twelve-year-old from her house based on a mailbox incident she hadn't witnessed? Tell Eli he couldn't be friends with someone because the HOA had opinions?

Kids did dumb things. That was the whole point of being a kid—you did dumb things, and hopefully adults helped you learn from them instead of writing you off.

She wasn't going to be that person. The neighborhood Karen who policed which children were acceptable. She'd met Tyler. He'd eaten her pizza and talked about video games and seemed like a perfectly normal kid.

Empty boat, she told herself. Don't fill it with a villain.

* * *

Two weeks later, 11:47 p.m.

Maeve was in bed, drifting toward sleep, when the explosion happened.

Not an explosion exactly—but that's what it sounded like. A rapid series of pops and cracks, loud enough to jolt her upright, heart pounding.

"What the hell?" James was already moving, out of bed, down the stairs.

She followed. Through the kitchen, out the back door, where the smell hit her first—smoke and sulfur, the acrid aftermath of fireworks.

The patio was covered in debris. Spent fireworks—blackened cardboard tubes, scattered paper, a few still sparking weakly in the dark. Half-eaten pizza slices, cheese congealing on the concrete. Empty soda cans. Chip bags. What looked like the remains of someone's party, dumped across their outdoor space and then set on fire.

"They're gone," James said, scanning the yard. "I saw them running, they went to Josh's house." The 12 year old that lived next door.

Maeve's stomach dropped.

"Are you sure?"

Josh. The neighbor kid, also friends with Tyler, also part of the pack that roamed the neighborhood looking for trouble.

Maeve stood on the patio, looking at the mess. The fireworks. The pizza. The trash.

Empty boat, she thought. *Don't fill it with a villain.*

But this wasn't an empty boat. This was her patio. Her space. Her home.

"I'm going over there," she said.

"Now? It's almost midnight."

"Yes. Now."

She didn't change out of her pajamas. Didn't fix her hair. Didn't remove the sleep mask that was pushed up onto her forehead like a headband. She just walked—across the yard, through the side gate, two houses down to Josh's place.

She knocked.

No answer.

She knocked again. Harder. Then again. She wasn't leaving.

Finally, footsteps. The door opened, and a teenage boy appeared—seventeen, maybe eighteen. Josh's older brother. He looked half-asleep and fully annoyed.

"Yeah?"

"I'm Maeve Campbell. I live next door. Your brother and his friends just set off fireworks on my patio and dumped trash everywhere."

The brother blinked, processing. "My parents aren't home."

"I can see that. Where are they?"

"At a party." He said it like this was normal. Like midnight on a weeknight with no adults home was just how things worked.

"Well, I need to talk to Josh. And Tyler. And whoever else is in there. Now."

The brother hesitated—weighing his options, calculating whether this woman in penguin pajamas with a sleep mask on her forehead was someone he could ignore.

Maeve didn't move. Didn't blink.

"JOSH!" the brother finally yelled over his shoulder. "Get out here. You're in trouble."

Shuffling. Whispered protests. Then Josh appeared,

and behind him Tyler, and behind him Jack. All of them caught. All of them knowing it.

"Mrs. Campbell says you dumped trash on her patio."

"I didn't—"

"Don't." Maeve's voice was calm but firm. "My husband saw you. You were with two other boys. You ran this direction. I'm not here to argue about whether it happened. It happened. I'm here because you're going to come back to my house right now and clean it up."

Tyler's face went through several expressions—denial, fear, calculation, and finally, defeat.

"Fine."

"Let's go," she said.

She walked them back to her house. Three twelve-year-olds trailing behind a woman in penguin pajamas with a sleep mask pushed up her forehead. She probably looked insane. She didn't care.

James had gotten brooms out. He handed one to each boy without a word.

"Every piece," Maeve said. "Every firework. Every pizza crust. Every chip. I want it cleaner than it was before you got here."

They swept. She supervised.

And while they worked, she talked.

"Here's the thing," she said, leaning against the patio door. "I don't think you're bad kids. I met you, Tyler. You sat in my kitchen and ate my food and talked about video games. You seemed fine. Normal. Like every other twelve-year-old."

Tyler didn't look up. Kept sweeping.

"But this?" She gestured at the mess they were cleaning. "This is a choice. This is deciding to make someone else's night worse for no reason. And choices have consequences."

"We were just messing around," Jack muttered.

"I know. That's exactly the problem. 'Messing around' means you didn't think about it. You didn't think about who would have to clean this up. You didn't think about the fact that real people live here—people who were sleeping, people who have to wake up early, people who didn't do anything to you."

She paused.

"I'm not going to yell at you. I'm not going to call you names. But I am going to tell you the truth: this is how it starts. Little stuff that doesn't seem like a big deal. Messing around. And then the little stuff becomes medium stuff, and the medium stuff becomes big stuff, and suddenly you're seventeen with a record and everyone's saying 'he was such a nice kid, what happened?'"

The boys were quiet. Sweeping.

"You have a choice right now. You can be the kids who did something stupid and learned from it. Or you can be the kids who did something stupid and kept going. That's up to you. Not me. Not your parents. You."

They finished sweeping. The patio was clean—cleaner than before, actually. James had been right to give them brooms.

"Thank you," Maeve said. "You can go."

They left quickly, not looking back.

James came to stand beside her.

"That was impressive," he said.

"I don't know if it'll make any difference."

"Maybe not. But you said what needed to be said."

Transparent and kind, she thought. *Both. Not one or the other.*

* * *

The next morning, Maeve sat with Eli.

He was at the kitchen table, eating cereal, reading a book. The same as every morning. But this morning felt different.

"We need to talk about last night," she said.

Eli's shoulders tensed. "I already heard."

"Then you know what Tyler and his friends did."

"Yeah."

"I don't want you hanging out with them anymore."

Eli looked up. "Mom—"

"I'm not saying they're terrible people. I'm not saying they can't ever change. But right now, they're making choices I don't want you associated with. And the thing about being twelve is that people judge you by who you spend time with. Fair or not, that's how it works."

"Tyler's not that bad. He just—"

"He dumped trash on our patio at midnight. Him and his friends."

"It was just a prank."

"It was disrespectful. And I saw how fast they ran

when your dad caught them. They knew it was wrong. They did it anyway."

Eli was quiet. She could see him wrestling with it— the loyalty to his new friends, the desire to belong, warring against the part of him that knew she was right.

"I'm not asking you to hate them," Maeve said. "I'm asking you to have better judgment than they do. You're a good kid, Eli. You're thoughtful and kind and you think about things before you do them. That's rare at your age. Don't let that get lost because you want to fit in with people who don't think at all."

Eli stared at his cereal.

"Can I at least still talk to them at school?"

"Of course. I'm not asking you to be rude. Just... don't be their partner in crime. Okay?"

He nodded slowly. "Okay."

She reached out, squeezed his shoulder. He let her.

"I know it's hard. I know you want friends. And you'll find them— the right ones. The ones who don't make you choose between being liked and being yourself."

Eli didn't say anything. But he didn't pull away either.

* * *

The question of what to do next lingered.

She'd made the boys clean up. She'd talked to them —transparent and kind, the best she could manage at midnight in penguin pajamas. She'd set a boundary with Eli.

But was that enough?

The HOA option loomed. Deborah would probably love to hear about this—more ammunition for her campaign against Tyler's family. Another incident for the file. Another reason to send letters, to threaten eviction, to make that family's life harder.

But something about it felt wrong.

Maeve thought about the empty boat. About the stories we tell.

Tyler wasn't a villain. He was a twelve-year-old with bad judgment and probably not enough supervision and the particular restlessness of boys that age who don't know what to do with their energy. The mailbox incident. The fireworks. The trash. These weren't the actions of a criminal mastermind. They were the actions of a kid who was bored and impulsive and hadn't learned yet that choices have consequences.

She'd tried to teach him that last night. Whether it landed, she had no idea.

Boys will be boys, people said. As if that explained anything. As if testosterone was an excuse for not raising your children to be decent humans.

But the opposite—treating every stupid kid decision as a criminal act, involving boards and letters and permanent records—that didn't feel right either.

Where was the middle ground?

James found her on the back patio that evening, staring at the spot where the trash had been.

"You're still thinking about it."

"Yeah."

"What are you going to do?"

"I don't know." She sighed. "I don't want to be a Karen. That word—it's everywhere now. Every time a woman speaks up about anything, she's a Karen. It's a way of silencing people. Of making us feel like any complaint, any boundary, any pushback is an overreaction."

"But?"

"But I also don't want to be a doormat. I don't want to 'boys will be boys' my way through this and then have them do something worse next time."

James was quiet for a moment.

"What's your gut say?"

She thought about it.

"My gut says I did what I needed to do last night. I addressed it directly. I made them clean up. I said my piece. Now it's on them to decide what they do with it."

"So you're letting it go?"

"I'm... watching. If it happens again, I'll escalate. But I don't think sending letters and involving the board for a first offense is the right call. They're kids. Kids mess up. The question is whether they learn from it."

James nodded. "That sounds reasonable."

"Does it? Or does it sound like I'm making excuses?"

"It sounds like you're trying to find the path that's firm but not cruel. That's not making excuses. That's being a grown-up."

She leaned into him. Let him put his arm around her.

"The empty boat thing," she said. "That's what I taught today. About not filling boats with villains."

"Is that what you're doing? Seeing Tyler as an empty boat?"

"I'm trying to. He's not a villain. He's just a kid in an empty boat, drifting into other people's lives, causing crashes. The crash happened. I dealt with it. Now I have to let go of the story I want to tell about who he is."

"That's generous."

"Is it? Or is it naive?"

"Maybe both. Maybe that's okay."

They stood there as the sun set, looking at the patio that was now cleaner than it had been in months.

"One more thing," Maeve said.

"What?"

"Eli. I told him he can't hang out with them anymore."

"Good."

"He wasn't happy about it."

"He's eleven. He's not supposed to be happy about boundaries. He's supposed to test them and complain about them and secretly be relieved that someone is paying enough attention to set them."

Maeve smiled. "When did you get so wise?"

"I've been listening to yoga teachers for fifteen years. Some of it stuck."

* * *

. . .

That night, lying in bed, Maeve thought about boats.

The boys in their empty boat, crashing through the neighborhood, not thinking about who they hit.

Tyler's mom, probably in her own empty boat—single parent, maybe struggling, definitely not fully aware of what her kid was doing at midnight.

Eli, in his boat, trying to figure out how to navigate the waters of middle school, desperate to find people who'd row alongside him.

James, in his boat. Steady, patient, sometimes distant. Still waiting for the conversation they kept postponing.

And herself. Her own boat. Drifting through days that blurred together, crashing into her children's needs, her husband's needs, her students' needs. Occasionally looking up and wondering where she was headed.

Most of it isn't personal, she'd said in class. *Most of it is just boats, drifting, occasionally crashing.*

But some of it was personal. Some of it required a response. The trick was knowing which was which.

She'd responded to the boys. Transparent and kind—or at least, transparent and firm. She'd set a boundary with Eli. She'd made a choice about how to move forward.

Now she had to let it go.

Empty boat, she told herself. *Let it be an empty boat.*

She tried.

Finn appeared in the doorway. Small footsteps padded across the floor. A small body climbed between them, already rotating toward his first position of the night.

"He's early tonight," James murmured.

"He's early every night."

"Should we—"

"Tomorrow," Maeve said. "We'll deal with that boundary tomorrow."

Finn's feet found her ribs. His body radiated heat.

She closed her eyes.

Tomorrow. There was always tomorrow.

Tonight, she'd done enough.

Tonight, she'd let the boats drift.

She slept.

5

Taste the Strawberry
Between the tigers, there is only this moment.

There's a story about a man being chased by a tiger.

Maeve stood at the front of the room, Saturday afternoon, 4 p.m.—the weekend class that drew a different crowd. People who worked during the week, who squeezed yoga into the margins of their lives. Twelve students today. Tired faces. Bodies that had been sitting in offices, hunched over keyboards, folded into car seats.

"He runs," she said, "until he reaches the edge of a cliff. There's nowhere to go. The tiger is behind him, snarling. So he climbs over the edge and grabs onto a vine."

She paused, letting the image build.

"He looks up. The tiger is pacing above, waiting. He

looks down. There's another tiger below, also waiting. And then he notices—two mice, one white and one black, are gnawing at the vine. It's going to break. It's only a matter of time."

The room was silent. Even the heaters seemed to hold their breath.

"And then," Maeve said, "he sees a wild strawberry growing from the cliff face. Right there, within reach. He plucks it. He puts it in his mouth."

She let the pause stretch.

"And it's the sweetest strawberry he's ever tasted."

A woman in the back row exhaled audibly. Someone else shifted on their mat.

"The tiger above is the past," Maeve continued. "Everything that's already happened, that we can't change, that chases us. The tiger below is the future—everything we're anxious about, everything we can't control. And the mice? The mice are time itself, gnawing away at this moment, this vine, this life."

She walked slowly through the room.

"We spend so much energy running from the past tiger. Worrying about the future tiger. Watching the mice with dread. And we miss the strawberry. The one thing that's actually here. The one thing we can actually taste."

She returned to the front.

"Today, the practice is tasting the strawberry. Not solving anything. Not fixing anything. Not planning or regretting or worrying. Just being here. Just tasting what's in front of you."

She guided them down to their mats.

"Let's begin."

The class unfolded slowly. Gentle stretches, long holds, breath awareness. Maeve kept the pace unhurried, the cues minimal. Space for people to actually be where they were instead of rushing to the next thing.

"Notice if you're already thinking about what comes after class," she said during a seated forward fold. "Dinner plans. Errands. The week ahead. That's the future tiger. See if you can come back to the strawberry. This breath. This stretch. This moment."

She watched the room. Saw the tension in shoulders that wouldn't release. The jaws that stayed clenched even in restorative poses. The particular restlessness of people who had forgotten how to be still.

She knew that restlessness. She lived inside it.

"The strawberry isn't always sweet," she added. "Sometimes the present moment is uncomfortable. Boring. Painful. The practice isn't about the moment being good. It's about being in the moment, whatever it is."

During savasana, she let them rest in silence. No music, no guided relaxation. Just the hum of the heaters and the sound of breath.

Taste the strawberry, she thought. *Even when the strawberry is just... this. Just lying on a mat. Just being alive. Just existing between tigers.*

It was harder than it sounded.

It was always harder than it sounded.

. . .

* * *

The text had come that morning.

Hey lady! A bunch of us are getting together tonight at Zoe's. Wine, cheese, catching up. You in? We miss your face!

It was from Jen. One of the mom friends from Sage's old school—back when Sage was in elementary and Maeve had been part of a group. Playdates that turned into wine nights. Birthday parties where the parents lingered long after the cake was cut. A community of women navigating motherhood together.

She hadn't seen most of them in months. Maybe longer.

Maeve stared at the text for a full minute before responding.

Ugh I wish! Can't tonight—already have plans. Rain check?

The lie was smooth. Automatic. She'd told it so many times it barely registered as a lie anymore.

The truth was she had no plans. James was home. The kids were occupied. She could absolutely go to Zoe's house, drink wine, catch up, be social.

She just... didn't want to.

The thought of it—the getting ready, the driving, the small talk, the being "on" for three hours—made her feel tired in her bones. Not the good tired of a full day. The preemptive tired of spending energy she didn't have.

What is wrong with me?

She used to be social. Used to crave connection, conversation, the warmth of being known by people who weren't her children or her husband. Used to count down the days until the next girls' night, the next dinner party, the next chance to be Maeve-the-person instead of just Maeve-the-mom.

Now the invitations felt like obligations. The friendships like one more thing to maintain. The social energy she used to have in abundance had dwindled to almost nothing, and what little remained, she hoarded like a miser.

Hermit, she thought. *You've become a hermit.*

And the worst part? She liked it.

She liked the quiet evenings at home. Liked the solitude of early mornings. Liked knowing she could have friends—could pick up the phone, could say yes to the wine night—but choosing not to.

Was that healthy? Or was she disappearing?

She didn't know. She wasn't sure she wanted to find out.

***

The nail salon with Sage happened on Sunday.

It wasn't planned—not really. Maeve had woken up thinking about strawberries, about presence, about the time that kept slipping past while she was busy watching the mice.

"Want to get our nails done?" she asked Sage over breakfast. "Just us?"

Sage looked up from her phone, suspicious. "Why?"

"Because I want to spend time with you. Just you. No brothers."

"Is this because of the acne thing? Are you trying to make me feel better about my face?"

"No. This is because you're my daughter and I like you and we never do anything just the two of us anymore."

Sage considered this. Maeve could see her running calculations—what was the catch, what was the agenda, what was mom really after.

"Okay," she finally said. "But I get to pick the color."

"You always get to pick the color."

"And you're not allowed to say anything about my phone usage while we're there."

"Deal."

"And you're paying."

"Obviously."

Sage almost smiled. "Fine. Let's go."

The nail salon was crowded—Sunday afternoon, everyone with the same idea. They sat side by side in massage chairs, feet soaking in warm water, while technicians whose names Maeve should have learned by now but never did prepped their stations.

Maeve's phone was in her purse. She'd left it there deliberately—no checking emails, no scrolling, no escaping into the screen. Just this. Just Sage. Just the strawberry.

"So," she said. "How are you? Really."

Sage glanced at her sideways. "You're doing the therapy voice."

"What therapy voice?"

"The 'how are you really' voice. Like you're waiting for me to have a breakdown."

Maeve laughed. "I'm not waiting for anything. I'm just asking."

"I'm fine."

"Fine fine? Or fine like you say when you don't want to talk about it?"

Sage was quiet for a moment. The massage chair hummed beneath them. Someone's phone was playing music too loudly three chairs down.

"School's okay," Sage finally said. "Maya's being weird but that's normal. My skin is..." She gestured vaguely at her face. "You know. The same."

"I'm not commenting on your skin."

"I know. I'm just saying." She picked at her cuticle. "I've been thinking about maybe doing track in the spring. But I don't know. It's a lot of time commitment."

"Do you want to do track?"

"I don't know. Maybe. I used to like running. Before everything got..."

"Complicated?"

"Yeah. Complicated."

Maeve nodded. Didn't push. Just let the silence sit.

"Mom?" Sage said, after a minute.

"Yeah?"

"Why don't you ever hang out with your friends anymore?"

The question caught her off guard. "What do you mean?"

"Like, you used to go out. With Jen and those people. Wine nights or whatever. Now you're always just... home."

Maeve felt something twist in her chest. Her fourteen-year-old had noticed. Had been paying attention to the absence she thought she'd hidden.

"I don't know," she said honestly. "I guess I've become kind of a hermit."

"Is that bad?"

"I don't know that either."

Sage considered this. "I think it's okay to not want to hang out with people. Sometimes I don't want to hang out with anyone. Like, I have friends, but sometimes I'd rather just be in my room doing nothing."

"That's normal at your age."

"Maybe it's normal at your age too."

"Maybe," she said. "Maybe it is."

The technician arrived, started working on Sage's feet. The conversation shifted to nail colors—Sage wanted something called "Vampire State of Mind," a deep burgundy that would definitely get comments at school. Maeve chose a neutral pink, boring and safe.

But something had loosened in her chest. The guilt

she'd been carrying about the canceled plans, the declined invitations, the slow retreat from social life—it felt lighter now. Not gone, but lighter.

Maybe it's normal at your age too.

Maybe.

* * *

The hike with Eli happened on Tuesday.

She'd picked him up from school and driven straight to the trailhead instead of home. He'd looked confused when she passed their street.

"Where are we going?"

"Hiking."

"Why?"

"Because I want to spend time with you. Just you."

He was quiet for a moment. Then: "Is this because of the Tyler thing? Are you checking on me?"

"No. This is because you're my son and I like you and we never do anything just the two of us anymore."

Eli considered this. Unlike Sage, he didn't argue or negotiate. He just nodded and went back to looking out the window.

The trail was easy—a loop through the hills, nothing strenuous. Late afternoon light filtered through the trees. The air smelled like eucalyptus and recent rain.

They walked in silence for the first ten minutes. Eli wasn't a talker—never had been. He processed the world internally, in ways Maeve couldn't always access. Pushing him to share only made him retreat further.

So she didn't push. She just walked beside him, matching his pace, letting the quiet be enough.

Eventually, he spoke.

"I've been reading about survival stuff."

"Yeah?"

"Like, what to do if you're lost in the wilderness. How to find water. How to build a fire. That kind of thing."

"Is this because of the island book?"

He looked surprised that she remembered. "Kind of. I've been reading more like it. There's this whole series about kids who survive plane crashes and stuff."

"That sounds intense."

"It's cool. They have to figure everything out themselves. No adults to help."

Maeve heard something underneath the words. A longing, maybe. For competence. For independence. For the ability to survive without needing anyone.

"Do you feel like you have to figure everything out yourself?" she asked.

Eli was quiet for a long moment.

"Sometimes," he finally said. "Like, everyone's always dealing with Finn's stuff or Sage's stuff. There's not really room for my stuff."

First arrow: her son felt invisible.

She waited for the second arrow—the guilt, the self-recrimination, the story about being a terrible mother who neglected her middle child.

It came. She let it pass.

"I'm sorry," she said simply. "That's not fair to you."

"It's okay. I don't really have that much stuff anyway."

"Everyone has stuff, Eli. Yours might be quieter, but it still counts."

He kicked a rock on the trail. Watched it skitter ahead.

"I like that you don't need me to fix things for you," Maeve continued. "But I don't want you to think that means I don't want to know what's going on. Your stuff matters to me. Even if I'm not always good at showing it."

Eli nodded slowly. "Okay."

"Okay."

They walked on. The trail curved upward, opening to a view of the valley below. They stopped, stood side by side, looked out at the hills and the houses and the distant smudge of the ocean.

"This is nice," Eli said.

"Yeah. It is."

"Can we do this again sometime?"

"Absolutely."

He didn't say anything else. But when they started walking again, he moved a little closer. Let his shoulder brush against her arm.

It was enough.

It was more than enough.

* * *

. . .

The indoor playground with Finn happened on Thursday.

This one required more energy—Finn at five was a tornado, a constant motion machine, a small human who experienced every emotion at maximum volume. Taking him anywhere was an exercise in endurance.

But she'd committed to the strawberry. To tasting it, even when it was loud and exhausting and covered in sticky fingerprints.

The playground was chaos. Screaming children, harried parents, the particular smell of sweat and rubber and spilled juice boxes. Finn disappeared into the climbing structure immediately, emerging only to shout updates.

"MAMA I'M ON THE THIRD LEVEL!"

"MAMA THERE'S A SLIDE THAT GOES IN A CIRCLE!"

"MAMA WATCH ME WATCH ME WATCH ME!"

She watched. Every time. Put her phone away and actually watched.

This is the strawberry, she told herself. *This moment. This child. This chaos.*

It didn't feel sweet. It felt overwhelming. But she stayed present anyway.

After an hour, Finn emerged, sweaty and grinning, and collapsed beside her on the bench.

"I'm hungry."

"I know. Let's get a snack."

"Can I get a pretzel?"

"Yes."

"With cheese?"

"Sure."

"And a slushie?"

"Don't push it."

He grinned. "Just the pretzel is fine."

They sat in the food court area—Finn inhaling his pretzel, Maeve nursing a coffee that had gone cold. Around them, other parents scrolled their phones, supervised half-heartedly, counted down minutes until they could leave.

Maeve kept her phone in her bag.

"Mama?" Finn said, through a mouthful of pretzel.

"Yeah, baby?"

"How come you're looking at me so much today?"

She laughed. "Because I like looking at you."

"But you usually look at your phone."

The observation hit harder than it should have. Her five-year-old had noticed. Had categorized her attention patterns. Had learned that Mama's eyes were usually somewhere else.

"I'm trying to be better about that," she said. "I want to look at you more."

Finn considered this, chewing. Then: "I like when you look at me."

"I like looking at you."

"Even when I'm being crazy?"

"Especially when you're being crazy."

He grinned, pretzel crumbs on his face, pure joy radiating from every pore.

This is the strawberry, she thought. *Right here. This face. This moment.*

The tigers were still there—the past and the future, the worries and the regrets. The mice were still gnawing. The vine was still fraying.

But right now, there was a pretzel. There was a grinning boy. There was this.

She tasted it.

* * *

That night, James found her on the couch.

The kids were in bed—all three, miraculously, including Finn, who had fallen asleep in his own room for once. The house was quiet in that particular way it only got after 9 p.m., when the chaos settled and the stillness felt almost sacred.

"You've been busy this week," James said, sitting beside her. "The nail thing with Sage. The hike with Eli. The playground today."

"I'm trying something."

"What?"

"Strawberries."

He raised an eyebrow.

"There's this story," she explained. "A man being chased by tigers, hanging from a vine, and there's a strawberry—"

"I know the story. You've taught it before."

"Right." She pulled her knees up, tucked her feet under her. "I've been thinking about strawberries. About presence. About how I'm always either running from something or worrying about something and I miss what's actually here."

"And the kids are the strawberry?"

"The kids are the strawberry. The time with them. The actual moments, not the managing of logistics. Does that make sense?"

"Yeah. It does."

They sat in silence for a moment. The refrigerator hummed. Outside, a car passed.

"Can I tell you something?" Maeve asked.

"Always."

"I've been feeling guilty. About being a hermit."

"A hermit?"

"I keep canceling plans. Saying no to things. I got a text from Jen this week about a wine night, and I just... didn't want to go. Made up an excuse. And then I felt terrible about it. Like something's wrong with me for not wanting to be social."

James was quiet, waiting.

"But then I was thinking about it," she continued. "About where my energy actually goes. And I realized—I'm not antisocial. I'm not disappearing. I'm just... spending it differently."

"On the kids."

"On the kids. On these one-on-one things. On actually being present instead of spreading myself so thin that no one gets anything real."

"That's not hermit behavior. That's just... priorities."

"Is it? Or am I just making excuses for becoming a recluse?"

James turned to face her. "Maeve. You teach fifteen classes a week. You talk to strangers constantly. You hold space for people's emotions as a literal job. And then you come home to three kids who need you in different ways at all times."

"So?"

"So maybe you don't need more social time. Maybe you need less. Maybe the wine nights aren't filling your cup—they're draining it. And the time with the kids, the one-on-one stuff? That's where you actually connect. That's where you're actually present. Why would you feel guilty about that?"

She stared at him.

"When did you get so insightful?"

"I've been watching you run yourself ragged for years. Eventually I started paying attention to what actually makes you happy versus what you think you should want."

"And what makes me happy?"

"Quiet. Solitude. Creative time. Deep conversations instead of surface ones. Being with people one at a time instead of in groups." He shrugged. "You're an introvert who somehow ended up with an extrovert's job. The hermit thing isn't a flaw. It's how you survive."

Maeve felt something release in her chest. Something she'd been carrying for months—maybe years. The guilt about not being social enough, connected enough, available enough. The story she'd been telling herself about being broken, being antisocial, being a bad friend.

"I think I needed to hear that," she said.

"I think you already knew it. You just needed permission to believe it."

She leaned into him. Let him put his arm around her.

"Three strawberries this week," she said. "One for each kid."

"Were they sweet?"

"They were. They actually were."

"Then that's enough. That's more than enough."

She thought about Sage at the nail salon, opening up about track. About Eli on the trail, admitting he felt invisible. About Finn with his pretzel, noticing that she was finally looking at him.

Three children. Three moments. Three strawberries.

The tigers were still there. The vine was still fraying. The mice were still gnawing.

But she'd tasted the strawberries. Really tasted them.

And James was right—it was enough.

It was more than enough.

* * *

Later, in bed, Maeve lay awake.

James was asleep beside her, breathing slow and steady. The house was quiet. Finn—miraculously—was still in his own room.

She thought about the week. The nail salon. The hike. The playground. Three children, three windows of undivided attention. Three strawberries.

She thought about the hermit thing. The guilt she'd been carrying. The invitations she'd declined, the friendships she'd let drift, the social life she'd slowly abandoned.

And she thought about what James had said: *Maybe you don't need more social time. Maybe you need less.*

It was permission she hadn't known she needed. Permission to be who she actually was instead of who she thought she should be. Permission to spend her limited social energy on the people who mattered most—her children, her husband, herself—instead of scattering it across obligations that left her empty.

She wasn't broken. She wasn't antisocial. She was just finite.

There was only so much of her to go around. And she was finally learning to spend herself wisely.

Taste the strawberry, she thought. *The one in front of you. Not the ones you think you should want. Not the ones everyone else is eating. Just the one that's actually here.*

Tomorrow there would be more chaos. More logistics. More running from tigers and watching mice.

But tonight, she'd had three strawberries.

And they had been sweet.

She closed her eyes.

She slept.

6

The Leaking Bucket

The crack in the bucket grew flowers along the path.

There's a story about a woman and two buckets.

Maeve stood at the front of the room, Wednesday evening, 6 p.m.—the after-work class that drew the exhausted, the depleted, the people who needed yoga most and had the least energy for it. Nineteen students arranged on their mats, still wearing the tension of their days.

"She carried water from the river to her house every day," Maeve said. "Two buckets, balanced on a pole across her shoulders. One bucket was perfect. The other had a crack in it."

She paused, letting the image settle.

"By the time she reached home, the cracked bucket was always half empty. And the cracked bucket felt terrible about this. Ashamed. It apologized to the woman constantly. 'I'm so sorry. I'm defective. You work so hard, and I leak out half of what you carry. You should replace me with a better bucket.'"

A woman in the front row was nodding. The one who always looked like she was apologizing for existing.

"But the woman just smiled," Maeve continued. "And she said, 'Have you noticed the path we walk every day? Look at your side of the path. Look at the other side.'"

She walked slowly through the room.

"On the perfect bucket's side—nothing. Dry dirt. But on the cracked bucket's side? Flowers. Wildflowers, growing all along the path. Because every day, the water that leaked from the crack watered the seeds. The bucket's flaw had created something beautiful."

Maeve returned to the front.

"The crack wasn't a failure. It was just a different kind of contribution. The bucket had been so focused on what it couldn't do—hold all the water—that it missed what it was actually doing. Growing flowers. Creating beauty. Being exactly what it was supposed to be."

She let that sit.

"Today, I want you to think about your cracks. The things you see as flaws. The ways you feel like you're not enough, not doing it right, not measuring up. What if those cracks are growing flowers? What if the thing you're apologizing for is actually creating something you can't see?"

She guided them to their mats.

"Let's begin."

The class unfolded gently. Restorative poses, long holds, lots of props. The kind of practice that asked nothing except presence.

"We spend so much energy trying to fix our cracks," Maeve said during a supported fish pose, hearts open to the ceiling. "Hiding them. Compensating for them. Apologizing for them. What if we just... let them be? What if we trusted that the leaking was doing something we couldn't understand?"

She thought about her own cracks. Her own apologies. The thing she'd been defensive about all week.

"You don't have to justify your existence," she added. "You don't have to earn your place by being perfect. The cracked bucket belonged on that pole just as much as the perfect one. It just did its job differently."

During savasana, she let them rest in silence.

The crack grew flowers, she thought. *Both things are true. The leak and the beauty. The flaw and the gift.*

She was still learning to believe it.

* * *

. . .

The corgi's name was Poppy.

She was ten weeks old, golden and white, with ears too big for her head and a tongue that seemed permanently extended. She cost more than Maeve wanted to admit—more than she'd ever spent on a dog, more than she'd spent on most things. A purebred from a breeder three states away, shipped on an airplane, delivered to her door in a crate with a bow on it.

Maeve had wanted a corgi her whole life.

Not instead of rescue dogs—alongside them. She'd fostered more dogs through the studio than she could count. Had a system: post the dog on social media, introduce them to students, find the right match. Her record was four dogs placed in under ten days each. She did fundraisers, organized donation drives, promoted rescue organizations on every platform she had.

But she'd always wanted a corgi. The stumpy legs, the fox face, the ridiculous waddle. She'd shown James pictures for years. "Someday," she'd say. "When we have room. When the timing is right."

The timing was never right. There was always another rescue that needed fostering. Always another dog that needed saving. Always a reason to put her own want aside.

Until last month, when she'd seen the listing. A breeder with a litter of corgis, one female left, available in six weeks. Before she could talk herself out of it, she'd put down the deposit.

"I'm getting a corgi," she'd told James that night.

"A rescue corgi?"

"No. A breeder corgi. A purebred."

He'd looked at her for a long moment. Then smiled. "Good for you."

"You don't think it's hypocritical?"

"I think you've rescued approximately four hundred dogs in the past five years and you're allowed to want something for yourself."

She'd almost cried. She hadn't realized how much she needed permission.

Poppy arrived on a Tuesday.

The other dogs were suspicious. Kona, the old lab mix, sniffed her once and walked away—too old for this nonsense, too tired to care. Mochi, the anxious golden, circled her nervously for an hour before deciding she wasn't a threat. Beans, the four-month-old chaos machine, immediately tried to play with her, which mostly meant jumping on her head repeatedly until Maeve intervened.

But by the end of the first day, they'd sorted themselves out. Four dogs. Three rescues and one purebred. A pack.

Maeve posted a photo on social media. Poppy in her lap, ears ridiculous, tongue out.

Meet Poppy. I've wanted a corgi my whole life. She's finally here.

The comments rolled in. Mostly positive. Heart emojis, congratulations, "she's adorable."

But then.

Don't you usually rescue dogs?

The comment was from someone she barely knew. A woman who came to class occasionally, who had opinions about everything, who had no filter and seemed proud of it.

Maeve stared at the words.

Don't you usually rescue dogs?

As if getting a purebred negated everything she'd done. As if one corgi erased years of fostering, fundraising, advocating. As if she wasn't allowed to want something just because she'd spent so long giving.

She typed a response: *Usually yes! But I've always wanted a corgi, so I splurged on this one. :)*

Friendly. Light. A smile emoji to soften any edge.

She hit send and tried to move on.

But the comment stayed with her. Lodged in her chest like a splinter.

* * *

The second comment came three days later.

Maeve was at the studio, setting up for morning class, when a student approached. A regular, someone she liked—warm, kind, genuinely curious about the world.

"I saw your new puppy on Instagram," the woman said. "She's so cute. Is she a rescue?"

The question landed differently than intended. Or

maybe it landed exactly as intended—Maeve couldn't tell anymore.

"No," she said. "She's a purebred. From a breeder."

"Oh." The woman's face did something complicated. Surprise, maybe. Or judgment. Or nothing at all—maybe Maeve was imagining it. "Well, she's adorable anyway."

Anyway.

As if being a purebred was something to overcome. As if Poppy needed a qualifier.

Maeve smiled. "Thanks."

The woman moved to her mat. Class started. Maeve taught on autopilot, her mind elsewhere.

Is she a rescue?

Did people ask that about every dog? Or just hers? Was she now the rescue dog lady, unable to make any other choice without explanation?

She thought about all the dogs she'd fostered. The ones she'd driven to vet appointments, nursed through illness, trained out of bad habits. The ones she'd photographed and promoted and placed in loving homes. The fundraisers she'd organized, the donations she'd solicited, the hours she'd spent advocating for animals no one else wanted.

And now, because she'd bought one purebred puppy, she was being questioned. Judged. Found lacking.

The crack in the bucket. The leak she couldn't stop apologizing for.

That night, Maeve did something petty.

She posted a carousel on social media. Ten slides. Every rescue dog she'd fostered in the past three years. Their names, their stories, the families who'd adopted them. Photos of fundraisers, screenshots of donation totals, testimonials from adopters.

So grateful for all the rescue babies who've come through our home and found their forever families. This work means everything to me. 🐾

She didn't mention Poppy. Didn't defend herself directly. Just... reminded everyone. In case they'd forgotten. In case they thought one corgi erased everything else.

James found her on the couch, scrolling through the comments.

"What are you doing?"

"Nothing."

"That's a lot of nothing." He sat beside her, looked at the screen. "Is this about the corgi comments?"

"No."

"Maeve."

She put down the phone. "Fine. Yes. It's about the corgi comments. Someone asked if I 'usually rescue dogs' like I'm some kind of hypocrite for getting a purebred. And then another person asked if Poppy was a rescue, like a ten-week-old corgi would somehow be in a shelter. And I just—" She gestured at the phone. "I wanted to remind people."

"Remind them of what?"

"That I'm not a monster. That I've done good things.

That I'm allowed to want something for myself without having to justify it."

James was quiet for a moment.

"You know you don't actually have to justify it, right? To anyone?"

"I know."

"Do you?"

She didn't answer.

"You got a dog you've wanted your whole life," James said. "That's allowed. You don't need to prove you've earned it. You don't need to list your credentials. You're allowed to just... want something. And have it."

"But people—"

"People are going to have opinions about everything. That woman with the comment? She probably didn't even think about it. It was just a thing she said. And the one who asked if Poppy was a rescue? She was probably just making conversation. You're the one turning it into a referendum on your character."

Maeve stared at him.

"When did you get so wise?"

"I've been paying attention." He took the phone from her hand, set it aside. "The post is fine. The rescue work is real. But you don't owe anyone an explanation for getting a corgi. The only person keeping score is you."

* * *

. . .

The next morning, Maeve woke early.

3:52 a.m. The house silent. She slid out of bed like goo—one limb at a time, slow motion onto the floor—and padded downstairs.

Poppy was in her crate in the kitchen, awake, tail wagging. Maeve let her out, took her to the yard, waited while she did her business. Then brought her to the couch, let her curl up in her lap.

This dog. This ridiculous, expensive, non-rescue dog.

She was perfect. Warm and soft and exactly what Maeve had always wanted.

The cracked bucket, she thought. *The one that grew flowers.*

Maybe the crack wasn't getting a purebred. Maybe the crack was needing everyone's approval. Needing to justify her choices. Needing to prove she was good before she was allowed to have something good.

She'd spent years pouring herself out for rescue dogs. And that was real—it mattered, it helped, it was part of who she was. But it didn't mean she wasn't allowed to keep something for herself. It didn't mean every choice had to be sacrificial.

The bucket leaked. The flowers grew. Both things were true.

She could be the rescue dog lady AND the woman with a purebred corgi. She could foster and fundraise and advocate AND buy the dog she'd always wanted. The crack didn't cancel the contribution. The splurge didn't erase the service.

She was allowed to hold both.

Poppy yawned, stretched, resettled in her lap.

You don't have to justify your joy, Maeve thought. *You don't have to earn every good thing. You're allowed to want something just because you want it.*

She was still learning to believe it.

But sitting here, in the early morning dark, with a corgi puppy snoring in her lap—she was closer than she'd been yesterday.

* * *

That afternoon, the woman with no filter came to class.

Maeve saw her unroll her mat in the second row—confident, oblivious, the kind of person who said whatever she was thinking without considering how it might land.

Don't you usually rescue dogs?

The comment had been rattling around in Maeve's head for days. Building a story about this woman. Filling the boat with a villain.

But watching her now—arranging her props, adjusting her ponytail, chatting with the person next to her—Maeve saw something different. Not malice. Just... cluelessness. A person who said things without thinking. A bucket with a crack, leaking words instead of water.

Maybe flowers were growing somewhere along her path too. Flowers Maeve couldn't see.

Empty boat, she thought. *Don't fill it.*

Class started. Maeve taught about cracks, about buckets, about the flowers that grow where we least expect them.

"We're so quick to see our flaws as failures," she said during a long forward fold. "But what if they're just... different contributions? What if the thing we keep apologizing for is actually creating something we can't see yet?"

The woman in the second row was listening. Head bowed, body folded, present.

After class, she approached Maeve.

"That was really good today," she said. "The bucket thing. I needed that."

Maeve smiled. "I'm glad."

"I always feel like I'm messing up. Saying the wrong thing. My husband says I have no filter." She laughed, self-deprecating. "He's not wrong."

Don't you usually rescue dogs?

"I think we all have cracks," Maeve said. "The trick is trusting that they're growing something good, even when we can't see it."

The woman nodded. "I like that. I'm going to try to remember that."

She left. Maeve stood alone in the empty studio.

The woman hadn't meant anything by the comment. Hadn't been judging or accusing. She'd just been... leaking. Saying something without thinking, the way she apparently did all the time.

And Maeve had spent a week building a story about

it. Defending herself against an attack that was never really an attack.

The bucket leaked. The flowers grew. Both things were true.

She thought about Poppy at home, probably chewing on something she wasn't supposed to. Her expensive, non-rescue, wanted-her-whole-life corgi.

She didn't need to justify her.

She didn't need to prove anything.

She just needed to let herself have something good.

* * *

That night, Maeve deleted the carousel post.

Not because it was wrong—the rescue work was real, the dogs were real, the contribution was real. But she'd posted it for the wrong reasons. As defense. As proof. As a preemptive strike against judgment that mostly existed in her own head.

She didn't need to prove her goodness to anyone.

James found her on the couch, Poppy in her lap, phone in hand.

"You deleted the post," he observed.

"Yeah."

"How do you feel?"

"Lighter. Dumber for posting it in the first place. But lighter."

"You're not dumb. You were defending something you love. That's human."

"I was defending something that didn't need defending. That's exhausting."

He sat beside her, reached over to scratch Poppy's ears.

"She's a good dog," he said.

"She's a great dog."

"Worth it?"

"Every penny."

They sat in silence for a moment. The house was quiet—kids asleep, other dogs settled in their spots. Just the two of them and a corgi puppy.

"I teach about this stuff," Maeve said. "The buckets and the cracks and the flowers. And then I forget to apply it to myself."

"That's also human."

"It's annoying."

"That too."

She leaned into him. Let him put his arm around her.

"I'm done justifying her," she said. "Poppy, I mean. She doesn't need a backstory. She doesn't need credentials. She's just my dog. I wanted her. I got her. That's enough."

"That's enough," James agreed.

Poppy sighed, burrowed deeper into Maeve's lap.

The bucket had a crack. The crack grew flowers.

Both things were true.

And for the first time in a week, Maeve stopped apologizing for either one.

. . .

* * *

Later, in bed, Maeve thought about cracks.

The rescue work and the purebred. The solitude and the social guilt. The boundaries she was learning to set and the ones she kept failing to enforce.

All cracks. All leaks. All flowers growing where she couldn't see them.

She thought about the woman with no filter, who didn't mean harm but caused it anyway. Who was probably lying awake somewhere, replaying her own words, wondering why people always seemed hurt by things she said without thinking.

She thought about herself at the keyboard, posting defensive carousels, needing everyone to know she was good. As if goodness could be proved. As if love required receipts.

You don't have to justify your joy.

The words echoed in the dark.

Tomorrow there would be more cracks. More leaks. More opportunities to either apologize for them or trust that flowers were growing.

She chose flowers.

Finn's door opened down the hall. Small footsteps. The familiar weight of a small body climbing between them.

"He's back," James murmured.

"He's back."

Finn arranged himself perpendicular, already rotating toward his first position. His feet found her ribs.

Another crack. Another thing she hadn't fixed yet.

But somewhere, she had to believe, flowers were growing.

She closed her eyes.

She slept.

7

The Forge

Transformation requires heat. There is no other way.

There's a reason blacksmiths work with fire.

Maeve stood at the front of the room, Friday morning, 9 a.m., the heat already building. This was a vinyasa class—stronger, faster, more demanding than her usual offerings. The kind of practice that asked something of you.

"You can't reshape metal at room temperature," she said. "It doesn't work. The metal resists. It stays exactly what it was. But add heat—real heat, uncomfortable heat—and suddenly transformation becomes possible."

She moved through the room, watching bodies settle into their mats.

"We don't like this. We want change without discomfort. Growth without struggle. We want the sword without the forge." She paused. "But that's not how it works. The heat isn't the obstacle to transformation. The heat IS the transformation."

She guided them to standing, arms raised.

"Today we practice being in the fire. Not escaping it. Not numbing out. Not wishing we were somewhere else. Just being here, in the heat, letting it do its work."

They began to move. Sun salutations, building warmth. The room would get hot—she'd turned up the infrared heaters, pushed the temperature past comfortable. By the end of class, everyone would be dripping. Everyone would have wanted to quit at least once.

That was the point.

"The forge isn't punishment," she said, flowing through chaturanga. "It's not something being done to you. It's something being done FOR you. The heat is how the metal becomes the sword. The pressure is how the coal becomes the diamond. You don't get transformed by staying comfortable."

She thought about her own forge. The heat she'd been avoiding. The conversation that had been building for months.

Are we okay?

Tonight. She'd promised herself. Tonight they would finally talk.

. . .

The class built in intensity. Standing poses held longer than usual. Balancing sequences that demanded focus. Core work that burned. Through it all, Maeve kept returning to the theme.

"Notice when you want to escape," she said during a long warrior two hold. "The urge to come out early. The story about why you can't do this. That's the moment the forge is working. That's exactly when you need to stay."

She watched the room. Faces strained with effort. Bodies trembling. The particular silence of people too focused to think about anything except the next breath.

"Staying in the fire doesn't mean ignoring your limits," she added. "It means knowing the difference between 'this is dangerous' and 'this is uncomfortable.' Danger, you leave. Discomfort, you stay. The growth is in the staying."

During the final pose before savasana—a long pigeon hold, hips releasing—she let them rest in silence. The heat wrapped around them like a blanket. The work was done. Now came the integration.

"The forge changes you," she said quietly. "But only if you let it. Only if you stay long enough for the heat to do its work. The sword doesn't resist the fire. It surrenders to it. And that surrender is what makes it strong."

She guided them down for savasana.

"Rest now. Let the heat settle. Let the transformation integrate."

She closed her own eyes.

Tonight, she thought. *We go into the forge tonight.*

. . .

* * *

The conversation with James had been building since January.

It had started with a text. A simple question in the middle of an ordinary Tuesday: *Are we okay? Like really okay?*

She'd read it in the school pickup line, Finn chattering in the backseat about something that happened at recess. She'd stared at the words for a long time before responding.

What do you mean?

I don't know. Just feeling disconnected lately. Like we're roommates running a household instead of partners.

Her chest had tightened. Because he wasn't wrong. She'd felt it too—the slow drift, the way they moved around each other without quite touching, the efficiency that had replaced intimacy.

Can we talk about it tonight?

Yes. Tonight.

But that night, Finn had a fever. And the next night, she'd had a late class. And the night after that, they were both too tired, and it felt easier to watch TV in silence than to open something they might not be able to close.

The conversation kept getting postponed. A week became a month. A month became three. The question hung between them, unanswered—*are we okay?*—growing heavier with each day they didn't address it.

They were fine. That was the thing. They weren't fighting. They weren't distant in any dramatic way. They still laughed together, still touched in passing, still functioned as a unit. From the outside, nothing was wrong.

But James had asked the question. Which meant something was wrong for him. Something she'd been too busy, too distracted, too wrapped up in her own survival to see.

Tonight, she would see.

* * *

The kids were in bed by 8:30.

A miracle, really. Finn had gone down without a fight —exhausted from a playdate, passed out in his own bed for once. Eli had retreated to his room with a book. Sage was doing homework, or pretending to, earbuds in.

The house was quiet. The dogs were settled. There was nothing left to do, no one left to tend.

Just them.

James was on the couch when she came downstairs. Not watching TV, not scrolling his phone. Just sitting. Waiting.

"Hey," she said.

"Hey."

She sat beside him. Not touching, but close. The

space between them felt charged—not with anger, but with the weight of things unsaid.

"So," she said.

"So."

A long pause.

"I've been avoiding this," Maeve admitted.

"I know."

"I'm sorry."

"I know that too."

She turned to face him. He looked tired—not sleepy tired, but the bone-deep tired of carrying something alone.

"Tell me," she said. "What you were feeling when you sent that text. What you're still feeling."

James was quiet for a moment. She watched him gather his thoughts, choose his words. He was always careful with words—unlike her, who wielded them like weapons when she was hurt.

"I feel like I'm disappearing," he finally said. "In this house. In this marriage. Like I'm useful—I'm helpful, I do things, I show up—but I'm not... seen. Does that make sense?"

It did. It made too much sense.

"I come home from work," he continued, "and everyone needs you. The kids, the dogs, the house. And I get it—I get that you're stretched thin, that there's not enough of you to go around. But sometimes I feel like I'm just another task on your list. Another person who needs something from you."

"James—"

"Let me finish." He said it gently, but firmly. "I'm not trying to make you feel bad. I'm trying to tell you the truth. You asked. This is the truth."

She nodded. Stayed quiet.

"When we first got together," he said, "you touched me all the time. Just... casual touch. A hand on my arm. Sitting close on the couch. Reaching for me in bed. And I know—" He held up a hand before she could interrupt. "I know touch isn't your thing. I know it doesn't come naturally to you. But it's my thing. It's how I feel loved. And somewhere along the way, it stopped."

Maeve felt something twist in her chest. She knew this about him. Had known it for fifteen years. And she'd let it slip anyway—let the chaos of kids and life and survival crowd out the thing he needed most.

"I'm not asking you to be someone you're not," James said. "I'm just asking you to try. To remember that I'm here. That I need something too."

The words hung in the air. Not accusatory. Not angry. Just honest.

Transparent and kind, she thought. *He's being transparent and kind.*

"Can I talk now?" she asked.

"Yeah."

She took a breath. "You're right. I've been treating you like a roommate. Like someone who helps with logistics instead of someone I chose. And that's not fair."

"It's not about fair—"

"It is, though. Because you show up for me. Every day. You listen to my yoga metaphors. You hold space when I'm falling apart. You're patient when I snap at you, which—" She laughed, humorless. "Which I do. A lot. I go for the jugular when I'm upset. I say the worst thing I can think of, and then I feel terrible, and then I apologize. And you just... take it. Every time."

"I don't take it," James said quietly. "I mope."

"You do mope. God, the moping." She smiled despite herself. "You get this look on your face, and you walk around the house like someone ran over your dog, and it drives me insane."

"Better than saying the worst thing I can think of."

"Is it? At least when I'm awful, it's out in the open. We fight, we apologize, we move on. When you mope, I have to guess what's wrong. I have to wait you out. I hate waiting."

"I know. That's why I mope." He was almost smiling now. "Because you hate it. Because it's the one thing that actually gets through to you."

"That's manipulative."

"It's strategic."

They looked at each other. The tension in the room had shifted—still serious, but lighter somehow. The honesty was doing its work.

"I'm sorry," Maeve said. "For not touching you. For treating you like a task. For going for the jugular and then expecting you to just get over it."

"I'm sorry for moping. And for not telling you what I need instead of just... hoping you'd notice."

"We're both bad at this."

"We're both learning."

She reached out. Took his hand. It felt deliberate in a way it hadn't in months—not automatic, not habitual, but chosen.

"Touch is hard for me," she said. "You know that. After a whole day of kids crawling on me and dogs needing walks and students needing adjustments—by the end of the day, I'm touched out. There's nothing left."

"I know."

"But that's an explanation, not an excuse. I can try harder. I can make sure something is left for you. I just need you to remind me. Not in a passive way—not moping—but actually telling me. 'I need you to hold my hand right now.' 'I need you to sit closer.' Can you do that?"

James nodded slowly. "I can try."

"And I need you to try harder with acts of service. That's my thing—you know that. When you empty the dishwasher without being asked, when you handle the kids so I can have five minutes alone, when you notice the thing that needs doing and just do it—that's how I feel loved. And lately..." She trailed off.

"Lately I've been slacking."

"A little."

"More than a little."

"Maybe."

He squeezed her hand. "I can try harder. I can be better about noticing. But you have to tell me too. Not in a critical way—not 'you never help' or 'why didn't you do this'—but actually asking. 'Can you handle bedtime tonight?' 'Can you clean the kitchen?' Give me the chance to show up instead of assuming I won't."

"I do that," she admitted. "Assume you won't. And then I resent you for not doing the thing I never asked you to do."

"Yeah. You do."

"That's not fair."

"No. But we're not keeping score anymore, remember? We're just trying."

She leaned into him. Let her head rest on his shoulder. His arm came around her—the touch she'd been denying him, the connection he'd been craving.

"Are we okay?" she asked. "Really?"

"I think so. I think we're better than okay. I think we just needed to say the things we've been not-saying."

"The forge."

"What?"

"That's what I taught today. The forge. How transformation requires heat. How you don't get the sword without the fire." She looked up at him. "This was our forge. This conversation. We've been avoiding it because it was uncomfortable. But the discomfort is how we get better."

James was quiet for a moment. Then: "Did you just turn our marriage into a yoga metaphor?"

"I turn everything into a yoga metaphor."

"I know. I love that about you."

"Even when it's annoying?"

"Especially when it's annoying."

She kissed him. Not a peck, not a habit—a real kiss.

The kind they used to share before kids and chaos and survival mode.

"I'm going to try," she said. "With the touch thing. I'm going to try harder."

"I'm going to try too. With the acts of service thing. With the telling you what I need instead of moping."

"We're going to mess up."

"Definitely."

"I'm going to go for the jugular at least three more times this month."

"Probably more."

"And you're going to mope."

"Almost certainly."

"But we'll apologize."

"Within twenty minutes."

"Usually less."

He pulled her closer. She let him. The touch she usually resisted felt different now—not a demand, but an offering. Not a taking, but a giving.

"I love you," she said. "I know I don't say it enough. I know I show it wrong half the time. But I love you. You're the person I chose. I keep choosing you."

"I love you too. Even when you're terrible."

"I'm frequently terrible."

"I know. I married you anyway."

They sat there, tangled together on the couch, the house quiet around them. The forge had done its work. They'd gone into the fire and come out the other side.

Not fixed. Not perfect. But closer. Clearer. More honest than they'd been in months.

. . .

* * *

Finn's door opened at 11:23 p.m.

They'd moved to the bedroom by then—not for anything dramatic, just lying together, talking in the dark about nothing and everything. The easy conversation that came after the hard one.

Small footsteps in the hallway. The creak of their door. A small body climbing up, arranging itself perpendicular between them.

"He's back," James murmured.

"He's back."

They looked at each other in the dark. The familiar weight of their son between them—the boundary they'd been "tomorrow"-ing for months.

"We should probably talk about this one too," Maeve said.

"Probably."

"Tomorrow?"

"Tomorrow."

Finn's feet found her ribs. His small body radiated heat.

Another forge. Another fire they weren't ready for yet.

But tonight, they'd done enough. They'd gone through one fire and survived. The sword was stronger for it.

Tomorrow there would be other fires. Other forges. Other transformations waiting in the heat.

For now, this was enough.

James reached across Finn's small body and found her hand. She let him take it.

Touch. His language. Her effort.

She squeezed back.

His language received.

They slept.

8

Kali
Destruction is creation wearing a different face.

Kali is not a gentle goddess.

Maeve stood at the front of the room, Saturday evening, 5 p.m.—the class she called "The Burn." Vinyasa with heat, intensity with intention. The students who came to this class knew what they were signing up for. They came to be destroyed.

"She's depicted with wild hair, a necklace of skulls, a skirt of severed arms," Maeve said. "She holds a sword in one hand, a severed head in the other. Her tongue is out, dripping blood. She dances on the corpse of her husband, Shiva."

A few students shifted on their mats. Kali made people uncomfortable. That was part of the point.

"In the West, we see this imagery and think: monster. Demon. Something to fear." Maeve shook her head. "But in the yogic tradition, Kali is the mother. The fierce, protective, terrifying mother who destroys what needs destroying so that new life can emerge."

She walked slowly through the room.

"The skulls around her neck? Ego deaths. The parts of ourselves we had to let go of to become who we are. The severed arms? Our attachments. The things we clung to that were keeping us small. The sword? Discernment. The ability to cut through illusion, through fear, through the stories we tell ourselves."

She returned to the front.

"Kali doesn't ask permission. She doesn't wait until you're ready. She comes when destruction is needed, whether you want it or not. And she burns everything that isn't true."

The room was silent. The heaters hummed.

"Today, we invoke Kali. We ask: what needs to be destroyed in my life? What am I clinging to that's keeping me stuck? What would I burn if I had the courage?"

She raised her arms overhead.

"Let's find out."

The class was relentless.

Sun salutations at a pace that left no room for thinking. Standing sequences that built heat upon heat. Balancing poses that demanded presence or punished distraction. Core work that burned, then burned some more.

Through it all, Maeve kept returning to Kali.

"She doesn't destroy because she's cruel," she said during a long chair pose, thighs shaking. "She destroys because she loves. Because she knows that some things have to die for other things to live. The caterpillar doesn't become a butterfly by adding wings. It dissolves. It destroys itself completely. And from that destruction, something new emerges."

She thought about her own destructions. The things she'd been avoiding burning. The conversations she'd been postponing.

"Kali energy isn't rage," she continued. "It's clarity. It's seeing what's true and acting on it, even when it's hard. Even when it hurts. Even when everyone else thinks you're being too much."

During a twisted lunge, she added: "Women especially are taught to soften our Kali. To be nice. To accommodate. To keep the peace at any cost. But sometimes peace isn't what's needed. Sometimes what's needed is a sword."

The class built to its peak—a challenging arm balance that most students couldn't hold, followed by a backbend that cracked open everything the heat had loosened. Then down, down, down into stillness.

"Kali's destruction always serves creation," Maeve said as they settled into savasana. "She doesn't burn for the sake of burning. She burns so new things can grow.

The question isn't whether destruction is coming—it always is, in one form or another. The question is whether you'll wield the sword yourself, or wait for life to wield it for you."

She let them rest.

Tonight, she thought. *Tonight I pick up the sword.*

* * *

The conversation started with Sage.

It was Sunday morning, the day after the Kali class. Maeve was in the kitchen, coffee in hand, when Sage appeared—still in pajamas, hair wild, face soft with sleep.

"Mom?"

"Yeah?"

"Can I talk to you about something?"

Maeve set down her coffee. Sage asking to talk was rare enough to warrant full attention.

"Of course. What's up?"

Sage sat at the kitchen table, pulled her knees up to her chest. Made herself small in that way teenagers did when they were about to be vulnerable.

"It's about Finn."

Maeve's stomach tightened. "Okay."

"I know this is going to sound mean. And I don't want to be mean. But..." Sage took a breath. "He's in your bed every night. And I know you think it's just a him-and-you thing, but it's not. It affects all of us."

"How do you mean?"

"Like—" Sage struggled for words. "Eli and I talk about it sometimes. About how Finn gets everything. Gets to sleep with you and Dad. Gets to break all the rules we had to follow. Gets all the attention because he's loud and we're not."

Maeve felt something crack open in her chest. "Sage..."

"I'm not saying you love him more. I know you don't. But it feels that way sometimes. Because Eli and I had to learn to sleep in our own beds. We had to learn to self-soothe or whatever. And Finn just... doesn't. And you let him."

The words landed like stones. Each one true. Each one heavy.

"I didn't realize you felt that way," Maeve said.

"I know. That's why I'm telling you." Sage looked up, eyes bright. "I'm not trying to get Finn in trouble. I just think—I think you need to know that it's not just about you being tired. It's about what's fair. And what we see. And what we're learning about how things work."

Maeve was quiet for a long moment.

Kali, she thought. *Destruction that serves creation. Truth that burns so new things can grow.*

"Thank you for telling me," she finally said. "That was brave."

Sage shrugged, but Maeve could see she was relieved. "Are you mad?"

"No. I'm grateful. You just held up a mirror I needed to see."

"So you're going to do something about it?"

"Yes. I'm going to do something about it."

* * *

Eli found her on the back patio an hour later.

She was sitting with Poppy in her lap, the other dogs sprawled around her feet. Thinking. Processing. Gathering courage.

"Mom?" Eli sat down beside her. "Sage said she talked to you."

"She did."

"Was she too harsh? She was worried she was too harsh."

Maeve shook her head. "She was honest. That's not the same as harsh."

Eli was quiet for a moment. Then: "I didn't want to say anything. Because it felt like complaining. And I know Finn is little and he needs more help. But..."

"But it doesn't feel fair."

"Yeah." He picked at a thread on his shorts. "When I was five, I had to stay in my own bed. Remember? You did that whole thing with the sticker chart. And I hated it, but I did it. And now Finn is five and he just... doesn't have to."

"You're right."

Eli looked up, surprised. "I am?"

"You are. I've been making excuses. Saying tomorrow, saying he's different, saying I'm too tired to fight it. But the truth is, I've been avoiding something hard because it was easier to just let it go."

"That's what you always tell us not to do."

"I know. I'm a hypocrite."

"You're not a hypocrite. You're just..." He searched for the word. "Human."

Maeve laughed—a real laugh, surprised out of her. "When did you get so wise?"

"I read a lot."

"That must be it."

They sat in comfortable silence. The dogs snored. A bird sang somewhere in the trees.

"I'm going to talk to him tonight," Maeve said. "Finn. About the bed thing."

"He's going to freak out."

"Probably."

"He's going to cry."

"Almost definitely."

"Are you ready for that?"

Maeve thought about Kali. About the sword of discernment. About destruction that serves creation.

"No," she admitted. "But I'm going to do it anyway."

* * *

. . .

The conversation with Finn happened at bedtime.

James was there—they'd agreed to do this together, united front, no cracks for a five-year-old to exploit. Finn was in his pajamas, teeth brushed, ready for the familiar migration from his bed to theirs.

"Buddy," James said, "we need to talk to you about something."

Finn's face immediately shifted to suspicion. "Am I in trouble?"

"No. You're not in trouble." Maeve sat on the edge of his bed. "But we need to make a change. Starting tonight."

"What change?"

"You're going to sleep in your own bed. All night."

The words landed. Finn's face crumpled.

"No."

"Yes."

"NO. I don't want to. I want to sleep with you and Daddy."

"I know you do. And we love sleeping with you. But you're five years old now. You're a big kid. And big kids sleep in their own beds."

"I don't WANT to be a big kid!"

"I know, baby. But you are one. Whether you want to be or not."

Finn's eyes filled with tears. Not the performative tears of a tantrum—real tears, genuine fear. Maeve's heart squeezed.

Kali, she reminded herself. *Destruction that serves creation. This is love. This is love wearing a different face.*

"I'll be scared," Finn whispered. "In the dark. By myself."

"You have your nightlight. And your stuffed animals. And we're right down the hall."

"But I want YOU."

"I know. And I want you too. But wanting something doesn't mean it's good for us." She brushed the hair from his forehead. "Do you know why we're doing this?"

He shook his head.

"Because you need to learn that you're okay on your own. That you can handle being alone in the dark. That you're brave and strong and capable, even when it feels scary." She paused. "And because your brother and sister had to learn this when they were your age. It's not fair that you haven't."

Finn's brow furrowed. "Eli and Sage had to sleep alone?"

"They did. And it was hard for them too. But they did it. And now they're not scared of the dark anymore."

Finn considered this. The tears were still there, but something else was working behind his eyes. The logic. The fairness argument. The realization that he wasn't being punished—he was being expected to grow up.

"What if I get scared?" he asked.

"Then you can hug your bear. Or turn on your light. Or think about all the brave things you've done. But you stay in your bed."

"What if I have a nightmare?"

James stepped in. "If you have a real nightmare, you

can come get us. But only for real nightmares. Not just because you want to."

"How will you know if it's real?"

"We'll trust you to tell us the truth."

Finn was quiet for a long moment. Then: "Will you stay until I fall asleep? Just tonight?"

Maeve looked at James. He nodded slightly.

"Just tonight," she said. "Tomorrow, we'll do a shorter time. And the next night, shorter still. Until you can fall asleep on your own."

"Like training wheels?"

"Exactly like training wheels."

Finn took a shaky breath. "Okay."

"Okay?"

"Okay. I'll try."

Maeve pulled him into a hug. Felt his small body against hers, warm and solid and so much braver than he knew.

"I'm proud of you," she whispered. "This is hard. And you're doing it anyway. That's what brave is."

"I don't feel brave."

"Brave people never do. They're too busy being scared to notice they're being brave."

She felt him smile against her shoulder.

***

She stayed until he fell asleep.

It took forty-seven minutes. Forty-seven minutes of lying beside him in the dark, feeling his body slowly relax, listening to his breathing shift from awake to asleep. Forty-seven minutes of resisting the urge to count, to calculate, to plan her escape.

She just stayed. Fully present. Watching her son learn to let go of her.

This is Kali, she thought. *This is the destruction that creates. The ending that allows a beginning.*

She'd been holding on too tight. Not just to Finn in her bed, but to the version of motherhood where she was always needed, always central, always the one they couldn't survive without. And that holding on wasn't serving anyone—not her, not James, not the older kids who'd noticed the unfairness, not Finn himself.

He needed to learn he could survive without her. And she needed to learn she could survive without being needed.

Both truths. Both necessary. Both Kali's sword, cutting through.

When his breathing finally deepened, when his limbs twitched the way they did when sleep had fully taken him, she slipped out of the bed. One limb at a time. Goo sliding off the mattress. Silent. Careful.

She made it to the door without waking him.

She stood there for a moment, watching him sleep. So small in his big-kid bed. So brave in ways he didn't recognize.

Goodnight, baby, she thought. *You're going to be okay. We both are.*

She closed the door softly behind her.

* * *

James was waiting in the hallway.

"He's out?"

"He's out."

"How do you feel?"

Maeve considered the question. How did she feel? Sad. Relieved. Proud. Guilty. Lighter. All of it, all at once.

"Like I just destroyed something," she said. "But in a good way."

"Kali?"

"Kali."

He put his arm around her. They walked to their bedroom together.

"What do you think happens at 2 a.m.?" James asked.

"I think he wakes up and comes to our room and we walk him back."

"And at 3 a.m.?"

"Same thing."

"And at 4?"

"Same thing. As many times as it takes."

"That sounds exhausting."

"It will be. For a while. And then it won't."

They climbed into bed. Their bed. Empty of children for the first time in months. The space felt strange—too big, too quiet. Maeve stretched her legs into the middle, reclaiming territory that had been occupied by small feet for so long.

"This is weird," she said.

"Good weird or bad weird?"

"Just weird." She rolled toward him. "I keep waiting for the door to open."

"It might."

"It probably will."

"And we'll handle it."

She rested her head on his chest. His hand came up to stroke her hair—the touch he needed, the touch she was learning to give.

"Thank you for doing this with me," she said. "I couldn't have done it alone."

"You could have. But I'm glad you didn't have to."

They lay in the dark, listening to the quiet. The house settling. The dogs snoring downstairs. The absence of small footsteps.

"Sage talked to me this morning," Maeve said. "About the Finn thing. About how it wasn't fair to her and Eli."

"What did she say?"

"The truth. That she and Eli had to follow rules Finn doesn't. That it affects them, even though they don't complain." She paused. "She held up a mirror. It wasn't fun to look into."

"But you looked."

"I looked. And then Eli said the same thing, in his own way. They've been watching. Noticing. Learning lessons I didn't mean to teach."

James was quiet for a moment. Then: "That's the thing about parenting. They learn from what we do, not what we say."

"I say that to my students all the time."

"I know. It's annoying when it applies to us, isn't it?"

She laughed softly. "Very annoying."

The silence stretched. Comfortable. Full.

"I love you," Maeve said. "For doing this with me. For being the kind of partner who shows up even when it's hard."

"I love you too. For being the kind of person who finally picks up the sword."

"Kali's sword."

"The very one."

She closed her eyes. Let the quiet hold her.

Destruction is creation wearing a different face, she thought. *The ending is the beginning. The burning is the growing.*

Tonight, she'd wielded the sword.

Tomorrow, the new growth would begin.

* * *

Finn appeared at 2:47 a.m.

Maeve heard the door creak, felt the shift in the room's energy. She was awake before his footsteps reached the bed.

"Finn."

"I waked up." His voice was small, trembling.

"I know. But remember what we talked about?"

"I stay in my bed."

"That's right."

"But I'm scared."

She sat up. Looked at him in the dark—small body, big eyes, fear radiating from every pore.

Kali, she reminded herself. *This is love. This is love wearing a different face.*

"I know you're scared," she said. "But you're also brave. And brave means doing hard things even when you're scared."

"I don't want to be brave right now."

"I know, baby. But I think you can be. I think you're braver than you know."

She climbed out of bed. Took his hand.

"Come on. I'll walk you back."

They padded down the hallway together, his small hand in hers. She tucked him back into his bed, adjusted his covers, placed his bear firmly in his arms.

"I'll be right down the hall," she said. "You're not alone. You're just... in your own bed. There's a difference."

"What's the difference?"

"Alone means no one cares about you. Your own bed means you're learning to be okay by yourself while people who love you are still nearby."

Finn considered this. "That's not as bad."

"It's not bad at all. It's just growing up."

She kissed his forehead. Stood to leave.

"Mama?"

"Yeah?"

"I love you."

"I love you too, baby. So much."

"Even when I'm not brave?"

"Especially when you're not brave. Because you're trying anyway."

She left the door cracked. Let a sliver of hallway light fall across his bed. Walked back to her own room.

James was awake.

"How'd it go?"

"He went back. He wasn't happy about it. But he went back."

"That's something."

"That's everything."

She climbed into bed. Stretched into the empty space. Let herself feel the strangeness of it.

"He'll come back again," James said.

"Probably."

"And we'll walk him back again."

"As many times as it takes."

"That's the job."

"That's the job."

They lay in the darkness, waiting for the next creak of the door, the next small footsteps, the next opportunity to be brave.

But the door stayed closed.

The footsteps didn't come.

And somewhere down the hall, a five-year-old boy was learning that he could survive the night on his own.

Destruction is creation, Maeve thought. *The burning is the growing. The ending is the beginning.*

She'd picked up the sword.

Now she had to trust what would grow from the ash.

She closed her eyes.

She slept.

9

Wash Your Bowl

Enlightenment is not somewhere else. It's in the dishes.

A student once approached a Zen master.

Maeve stood at the front of the room, Monday morning, 9 a.m., the start of a new week. Twenty-four students arranged on their mats, still carrying the weekend in their bodies—some relaxed, some tense, all of them showing up.

"The student asked: 'Master, what is the path to enlightenment? How do I find peace? How do I transcend this ordinary life and touch something sacred?'"

She paused, letting the question hang.

"The master looked at him and asked: 'Have you eaten your breakfast?'"

A few students smiled. They knew this story, or sensed where it was going.

"The student was confused. 'Yes,' he said. 'I've eaten.' And the master replied: 'Then go wash your bowl.'"

Maeve walked slowly through the room.

"That's it. That's the whole teaching. The student came looking for something extraordinary—a secret practice, a hidden truth, a path to transcendence. And the master pointed him back to the most ordinary thing imaginable. The dirty bowl. The task right in front of him. The thing he was avoiding because it wasn't special enough."

She returned to the front.

"We do this constantly. We chase peak experiences. We wait for the retreat, the breakthrough, the moment when everything will finally click. And meanwhile, the dishes pile up. The emails go unanswered. The bills sit unopened on the counter." She paused. "We think the sacred is somewhere else. But the master is telling us: it's right here. In the bowl. In the washing. In the ordinary, unglamorous, unsexy work of being a human in a life."

She guided them to seated position.

"Today, we practice washing the bowl. Not escaping into something higher. Not waiting for something better. Just being here, with what's in front of us, doing the next thing that needs to be done."

She brought her hands to her heart.

"Let's begin."

. . .

The class was simple. Grounding. Nothing flashy—just the basics done well. Standing poses held with attention. Forward folds that asked for presence. Twists that wrung out the weekend.

"Notice when you want to skip ahead," Maeve said during a long warrior one hold. "When you're already thinking about the next pose, the end of class, what you're doing after. That's the student asking about enlightenment while the bowl sits dirty in the sink."

She moved through the room, adjusting, offering cues.

"The bowl isn't going anywhere. The task doesn't disappear because you ignore it. It just sits there, waiting. Getting crusty. Harder to clean the longer you wait."

During a seated forward fold, she added: "Some of you are avoiding something right now. Something mundane. Something boring. Something that feels too small to matter but keeps nagging at the back of your mind." She paused. "That's your bowl. That's the practice calling you. Not the glamorous practice. The real one."

She thought about her own bowls. The stack of them, unwashed, growing higher by the day.

"Enlightenment isn't somewhere else," she said as they moved toward savasana. "It's not waiting for you on a mountaintop or in a silent retreat or after you've finally gotten your life together. It's here. Now. In the dishes. In the emails. In the thing you keep putting off because it's not special enough to deserve your attention."

She let them rest.

Wash your bowl, she told herself. *It's time to wash all the bowls.*

* * *

The stack of mail had been growing for three weeks.

It lived on the kitchen counter, in a basket Maeve had optimistically labeled "TO DO." Bills, school notices, insurance statements, things that required action. She walked past it every day. Acknowledged it with a glance, a twinge of guilt, a promise to deal with it later.

Later never came.

There was always something more interesting. More urgent. More alive than sitting down with a pile of paper and a checkbook and the grim reality of numbers.

But today was the day. She'd promised herself. After teaching about bowls all morning, she couldn't avoid her own any longer.

She poured a cup of coffee. Sat at the kitchen table. Pulled the basket toward her.

The first envelope was the tuition bill.

She'd known it was there. Had seen the school's logo in the corner, felt her stomach clench, shoved it to the bottom of the pile. But here it was, surfacing, demanding attention.

She opened it.

$5,400. Due in two weeks. Three kids, three tuitions, one impossible number.

She stared at it for a long moment. Then set it aside and kept going.

Electric bill. Water bill. The insurance premium that had gone up again. A notice from the dentist about Eli's missed cleaning. A letter from the HOA about some landscaping violation she didn't remember committing.

Each envelope was its own small violence. Each one a reminder of all the ways adult life demanded to be fed—constantly, endlessly, without regard for whether you had anything left to give.

By the time she reached the bottom of the pile, she'd written four checks, scheduled three appointments, and responded to two emails that had been flagged "urgent" for over a month.

The basket was empty.

The counter was clear.

And she felt—lighter. Not happy, exactly. But unburdened. The way you feel after finally ripping off a bandaid you've been picking at for weeks.

That's it, she thought. *That's the whole teaching. The thing you're avoiding isn't as bad as the avoiding itself.*

* * *

The money conversation happened that night.

She'd laid out the bills on the kitchen table—all of

them, organized by due date, amounts circled in red. James sat across from her, beer in hand, looking at the numbers with the particular expression of a man who knew this conversation was coming.

"We need to talk about spending," Maeve said.

"I know."

"We make good money. Both of us. But we also spend like we make more than we do."

"I know that too."

She gestured at the spread. "Tuition alone is $5,400 a month. That's $64,800 a year. Just to send our kids to school."

"When you say it like that—"

"It sounds insane. Because it is insane. And on top of that, we've got the mortgage, the car payments, insurance, utilities, groceries—" She stopped. "And then there's everything else."

James took a long sip of his beer. "Everything else?"

"The corgi."

"Poppy was—"

"Worth it. I know. I'm not saying she wasn't. But she cost more than our first car."

"Our first car was a piece of crap."

"That's not the point." Maeve pulled out her phone, opened the banking app. "I went through last month's statements. Do you want to know how much we spent eating out?"

"Probably not."

"$847. That's just restaurants. Not groceries. Restaurants."

James winced.

"And Starbucks. Between me and the kids, we spent $312 at Starbucks last month. That's ten dollars a day. On coffee and cake pops."

"The cake pops are non-negotiable. Finn will riot."

"I'm not saying never. I'm saying not every day. Not as a bribe every time I yell at them in the morning."

She scrolled further.

"Amazon. $634. And I couldn't tell you what half of it was. Just... stuff. Things I ordered at 11 p.m. because I was tired and it felt like self-care."

"Retail therapy."

"Expensive therapy. That doesn't actually work."

James set down his beer. "Okay. So what do we do?"

"We make a budget. A real one. And we actually stick to it."

"We've tried that before."

"And we've failed before. But we try again." She reached across the table, took his hand. "I'm not saying we become monks. I'm not saying no more fun, no more vacations, no more random hotel nights just because we feel like it. I'm saying we have to be intentional. We have to choose."

"Choose what?"

"Everything. Every time we spend money, we're choosing that thing over something else. Over the tuition. Over the savings we don't have. Over the retirement we're not funding." She paused. "I want to keep choosing vacations and nice dinners and the occasional splurge. But I also want to stop choosing without thinking. Stop swiping the card because it's easy. Stop avoiding the bills because looking at them feels bad."

James was quiet for a moment. Then: "The bowl."

"What?"

"That's what you taught today, right? Wash your bowl. Do the thing you're avoiding. The dishes don't disappear just because you don't want to do them."

Maeve stared at him. "You listened to my class?"

"Sage was telling me about it. She said it was about doing boring stuff instead of waiting for life to be exciting." He shrugged. "Sounds like a budget conversation to me."

"It is. It's exactly a budget conversation." She squeezed his hand. "The money stuff—it's my bowl. I hate it. I avoid it. I let it pile up until it feels insurmountable. And then I feel stressed all the time, and I don't even know why, because I won't look at the actual numbers."

"So we look at them."

"We look at them. Together. Every month. Like grown-ups."

"That sounds terrible."

"It does. But I think it'll feel better than avoiding it."

James finished his beer. Looked at the bills spread across the table. Sighed.

"Okay. Let's make a budget."

"Yeah?"

"Yeah. But I want it on record that I'm doing this under protest."

"Noted."

"And I reserve the right to complain the entire time."

"I would expect nothing less."

They pulled out a notebook. Started listing categories. Mortgage. Utilities. Tuition. Groceries. Gas. The essential stuff. The non-negotiables.

Then the other column. The choices.

"Eating out," Maeve said. "What's reasonable?"

"Once a week? As a family?"

"That's four dinners a month. At, what, $80-100 each? Call it $400."

"Half what we spent last month."

"Progress."

They kept going. Starbucks: twice a week max, not daily. Amazon: a 24-hour rule—nothing gets ordered the same night you put it in the cart. Target: avoid entirely if possible, because neither of them could walk in for toilet paper and leave without spending $200.

"What about vacations?" James asked.

"One big one a year. Planned in advance. Saved for."

"And the random hotel nights?"

Maeve hesitated. Those nights—the spontaneous escapes, the "let's just get out of here" weekends—they were her favorite indulgence. The way she survived the relentless grind of daily life.

"Quarterly," she said finally. "Four times a year. Budgeted."

"That's reasonable."

"It's less than we do now. But it's sustainable."

They finished the budget around 10 p.m. It wasn't perfect—there were categories they'd probably underestimated, expenses they'd forgotten. But it was something. A framework. A bowl, finally washed.

"How do you feel?" James asked.

"Like I just did something I've been avoiding for years."

"Good avoiding or bad avoiding?"

"Bad. Definitely bad. But it's done now." She looked at the notebook, the numbers, the evidence of their life reduced to columns and categories. "It's not as scary when you look at it. When you actually face it instead of letting it loom in the background."

"The bandaid thing."

"Exactly. Ripping it off hurts for a second. But then it's just... done. And you wonder why you waited so long."

James stood, started gathering the bills into a neat stack. "So we're doing this? Actually doing this?"

"We're doing this."

"No more late-night Amazon?"

"No more late-night Amazon."

"No more $43 Starbucks runs because you yelled at the kids?"

"I make no promises about the yelling. But I'll find cheaper ways to apologize."

He laughed. Pulled her into a hug.

"I'm proud of you," he said. "For facing the bowl."

"I'm proud of us. For doing it together."

They stood in the kitchen, holding each other, the budget notebook on the table behind them. Not a romantic evening. Not exciting or special or Instagram-worthy. Just two adults doing the boring work of being responsible.

Wash your bowl, Maeve thought. *This is it. This is the practice. Not the peak experience. The dishes.*

* * *

The next morning, Maeve called the dentist.

Eli's missed cleaning—rescheduled.

Then the accountant. The one she'd been avoiding for six months, ever since he'd mentioned something about quarterly taxes that made her want to crawl under the table and hide.

"I need to set up a meeting," she told the receptionist. "As soon as possible."

"We have an opening Thursday at 2."

"I'll take it."

Then the car. The safety check that had been overdue for—she didn't want to think about how long. She drove to the inspection station, waited in line, handed over the keys. Forty-five minutes later, she had a sticker. Legal. Done.

Three bowls, washed before noon.

Each one had felt impossible in the abstract. Each one had loomed large in her mind, growing more daunting the longer she avoided it. But the actual doing —the calling, the scheduling, the showing up—had been almost anticlimactic. Just tasks. Just steps. Just the ordinary work of being an adult.

Have you eaten your breakfast? Then go wash your bowl.

She understood it now. Not as a metaphor, but as a practice. The enlightenment wasn't in the avoidance. It wasn't in the waiting for conditions to be perfect, for energy to be available, for the stars to align. It was in the doing. In the facing. In the ripping off of bandaids that had been hanging by a thread for months.

She drove home with the windows down, something light in her chest that hadn't been there in a long time.

This, she thought. *This is what freedom feels like. Not the absence of responsibility. The completion of it.*

* * *

That night, she didn't order anything from Amazon.

She felt the urge—the familiar pull toward the app, the soothing scroll through things she didn't need but might want. The cart was still there, waiting. Thirteen items she'd added over the past week, totaling $247.

She looked at it. Really looked.

A sweater she didn't need but liked. A kitchen gadget that promised to solve a problem she didn't really have. Three books she could get from the library. Dog toys Poppy would destroy in five minutes. Stuff. Just... stuff.

She closed the app.

Didn't buy any of it.

The urge didn't disappear. It sat there, pulsing, wanting to be fed. But she didn't feed it. She let it sit. Let it be uncomfortable. Let herself feel the want without acting on it.

This is the practice, she thought. *Not getting rid of the want. Just not letting it run the show.*

She texted James: *Didn't order anything tonight. 24-hour rule.*

He texted back: *Proud of you. I almost bought a drill I don't need. Closed the tab instead.*

We're doing it.

We're doing it.

She smiled. Put down the phone. Picked up a book instead—one she already owned, one that had been sitting on her nightstand for months, waiting to be read.

The bowl was washed.

Now she could enjoy what she already had.

* * *

Finn slept in his own bed again.

Three nights in a row now. He still woke up—2 a.m., 4 a.m., the witching hours when the dark felt too big and his room felt too small. But he was staying. Fighting through it. Learning that he could survive the night alone.

Maeve walked him back each time. Tucked him in. Told him he was brave.

"I don't feel brave," he said, the same thing he said every night.

"Brave people never do."

She was starting to believe it herself.

The budget was pinned to the refrigerator. Visible. Unavoidable. A reminder that they were trying, that they were paying attention, that they were making choices instead of defaulting to habit.

The stack of mail was gone. The basket labeled "TO DO" sat empty on the counter—a small victory, but a real one.

The accountant meeting was scheduled. The car was legal. The dentist appointment was on the calendar.

Bowls. All of them washed. One at a time.

Later, in bed, James reached for her.

She let him. Turned toward him. Let herself be held.

"You did good this week," he said.

"We did good."

"The budget. The bills. The whole... adult thing."

"It's not sexy."

"No. But it's something. It's real."

She pressed her face into his shoulder. Breathed him in.

"I've been avoiding this stuff for years," she said. "The money, the appointments, the boring grown-up tasks. I kept waiting until I felt ready. Until I had enough energy. Until conditions were perfect."

"And?"

"And conditions are never perfect. And the waiting just made everything worse." She pulled back, looked at him. "The bowl doesn't care if you're ready. It just needs to be washed."

"Profound."

"Shut up."

"No, I mean it. Very wise. Very yoga teacher of you."

She hit him with a pillow. He laughed. Pulled her close again.

"I'm proud of us," he said. "For doing the hard stuff."

"The boring stuff."

"Same thing, sometimes."

She thought about the week. The bills, the budget, the phone calls she'd been dreading. None of it had been fun. None of it had felt spiritual or meaningful or Instagram-worthy. It had just been... necessary. The dishes that needed washing. The bowls that couldn't be ignored any longer.

Have you eaten your breakfast?

Yes. She'd eaten. She'd lived another day. She'd consumed resources and created messes and moved through a life that required maintenance.

Then go wash your bowl.

She was washing them. Finally. One at a time.

Not because she was ready. Not because conditions were perfect. Not because the task had become appealing.

Just because it was time.

Just because the bowl was dirty.

Just because the washing was the practice, and the practice was the point.

She closed her eyes.

Tomorrow there would be more bowls. More messes. More ordinary, unglamorous tasks that needed doing.

But tonight, she'd done enough.

Tonight, the bowl was clean.

She slept.

10

The Mustard Seed
You are not alone in your suffering.

There was a woman named Kisa Gotami who lived in ancient India.

Maeve stood at the front of the room, Sunday morning, 9 a.m.—the class that drew the seekers. The ones who came not just for the stretch but for the meaning. Fourteen students arranged on their mats, faces soft with weekend slowness.

"She married young," Maeve said. "Had one son. Her life was full of joy. But when the boy was old enough to run and play, he fell ill and died."

She let the words land.

"Kisa Gotami was shattered. She couldn't accept it. She carried his small body through the village, begging for medicine, certain there must be a cure. The villagers thought she'd gone mad. But one kind man said, 'I cannot help you, but the Buddha can. Go to him.'"

Maeve walked slowly between the mats.

"She found the Buddha and laid her son's body at his feet. 'Please,' she begged, 'give me medicine to bring back my child.' And the Buddha looked at her with infinite compassion and said, 'I will help you. But first, you must bring me a mustard seed from a house that has never known death.'"

A woman in the second row shifted. Linda. Maeve had noticed her come in—slower than usual, careful with her movements, something different in her eyes.

"Kisa Gotami was overjoyed. Mustard seeds were common—every household had them. She went to the first house. 'Do you have a mustard seed?' 'Yes,' they said. 'Has anyone in this house ever died?' The woman's face fell. 'Oh, my dear. My husband died just last year.'"

Maeve returned to the front.

"She went to the next house. And the next. And the next. At every door, the same story. A child lost. A parent buried. A sibling gone too soon. Every single house had known death. Not one was untouched."

She paused.

"And slowly, Kisa Gotami understood. She was not alone. Her grief was not singular. Every home, every family, every heart had been touched by loss. Suffering was not her private burden—it was the shared condition of being human."

Maeve looked at her students. At Linda, who wouldn't meet her eyes.

"She buried her son and returned to the Buddha. 'I understand now,' she said. And she became one of his most devoted disciples. Not because her grief disappeared—but because her isolation did. She was no longer alone with her pain. She was connected to every other grieving heart that had ever beaten."

Maeve brought her hands together at her chest.

"Today, whatever you carry—grief, loss, fear, worry—I want you to remember: you are not alone. Someone else has felt this. Someone else is feeling it right now, somewhere in the world. Your pain doesn't separate you from humanity. It connects you to it."

She guided them to their mats.

"Let's begin."

The class moved gently. Maeve had planned a hip-and-heart-focused practice—long holds, lots of props, space for whatever needed to surface.

In butterfly pose, she walked the room, adjusting a bolster here, offering a blanket there. When she reached Linda, she knelt beside her.

"How are you doing?" Maeve asked softly, placing a block under Linda's knee.

Linda's eyes welled. "I'm okay."

She wasn't okay. Maeve could see it. But class wasn't the place to push.

"I'm here if you need anything."

Linda nodded, tears sliding down her temples into her hair.

Maeve moved on, continuing her rounds, but her attention kept returning to the second row. To Linda's careful breathing. To the way she held her chest, protective, guarded.

After class, students rolled their mats, gathered their things, filtered out with soft goodbyes. Linda stayed. She sat on her mat, knees hugged to her chest, staring at nothing.

Maeve waited until the room was empty, then sat down beside her.

"Hey."

Linda looked up. Her face was blotchy, eyes red. "I'm sorry. I don't know why I can't stop crying."

"You don't have to apologize for crying. Not here."

"It's just—" Linda pressed her hands to her chest. "I found out last week. I have to have surgery. My heart. There's something wrong with a valve. They said it's routine, but—"

Her voice broke.

"But it doesn't feel routine," Maeve finished.

"No." Linda shook her head. "It feels like everything might end. Like I've been walking around my whole life assuming my heart would just... keep going. And now I know it might not. That it almost didn't."

Maeve sat with her. Didn't rush to fill the silence.

"When is the surgery?"

"Three weeks. They wanted to do it sooner, but I asked them to wait. I have a trip planned with my daughter. We've been planning it for two years. I know it's stupid—"

"It's not stupid."

"They said I shouldn't go. That I should rest. But I keep thinking—what if something goes wrong? What if I never get another chance to take her to Paris?"

Maeve felt the weight of the question. The impossible math of it. Rest versus risk. Safety versus living.

"What does your gut say?"

Linda laughed, a wet, broken sound. "My gut says go. My gut says I've spent my whole life being careful, doing the responsible thing, and where did it get me? A faulty valve and a surgery date."

"Then maybe your gut is right."

"But what if—"

"There's always a what if. There's always a tiger behind you and a tiger below." Maeve smiled. "You know that story. The man on the vine. Sometimes you just have to taste the strawberry."

Linda wiped her face. "I came to class today because I didn't know where else to go. I haven't told anyone except my husband. I don't want people to look at me differently. To treat me like I'm fragile."

"You're not fragile. You're human. There's a difference."

"Is there?"

Maeve considered the question. "Fragile means you break easily. Human means you break—and you keep going anyway. You're here. On your mat. Three weeks before heart surgery. That's not fragile. That's brave."

Linda's face crumpled again. But this time, something in her softened. The rigid holding in her chest loosened, just slightly.

"The Mustard Seed story," she said. "I kept thinking about it during class. Every house has known death. Every heart has been touched by loss."

"Every heart."

"Even yours?"

Maeve nodded. "Even mine."

She didn't elaborate. Didn't list her own losses, her own fears, the nights she'd lain awake wondering if her own heart would keep beating. This wasn't about her. It was about Linda. About being present for someone else's suffering without trying to fix it or match it.

"I'm scared," Linda whispered.

"I know."

"What if I don't make it?"

"Then you'll have gone to Paris with your daughter. You'll have tasted the strawberry. You'll have lived."

"And if I do make it?"

Maeve smiled. "Then you'll have a hell of a story. And a new valve. And the rest of your life."

Linda laughed again, lighter this time. She reached out and squeezed Maeve's hand.

"Thank you. For sitting with me. For not trying to make it better."

"Some things can't be made better. They can only be witnessed."

"That should be on a bumper sticker."

"I'll pitch it to marketing."

They sat for another moment, the empty studio quiet around them. The smell of sweat and incense. The late morning light through the windows.

Finally, Linda stood. Gathered her things. At the door, she turned back.

"I'll be here next Sunday. Before I leave for Paris."

"I'll save your spot."

Maeve cleaned the studio alone. Sprayed the mats, wiped down the props, straightened the bolsters against the wall. Mechanical tasks. The kind that let your mind wander.

She thought about Linda's heart. About the valve that had been failing, quietly, invisibly, while Linda went about her life—making dinner, doing laundry, planning trips to Paris. The body carrying its own secrets. Its own ticking clocks.

She thought about her own heart. The one that had been racing lately, skipping beats when she was tired. She'd chalked it up to stress. To the kids. To the endless hamster wheel of motherhood and business ownership and trying to be present for everyone while running on empty.

But what if it wasn't just stress?

She pushed the thought away. Focused on the mats. On the rhythm of spray-wipe-stack.

Her phone buzzed. James.

Kids want tacos. I'm taking them to the truck. You want your usual?

She smiled. Her usual. Fish tacos, extra lime, cabbage on the side. The fact that he knew that—still knew that, after fifteen years—felt like its own kind of miracle.

Yes please. Home in 20.

She finished the mats. Turned off the lights. Locked the door.

In the parking lot, she paused. Looked up at the sky—bright blue, winter sharp, the kind of day that felt like a gift. She breathed in. Breathed out.

Every house has known death. Every heart has been touched by loss.

But not today. Today, her heart was beating. Her children were eating tacos. Her husband knew her order.

Today, the mustard seed was just a story.

She got in her car and drove home.

That night, after tacos and homework and the endless negotiations of bedtime, Maeve sat on the lanai with James. The kids were finally asleep—Sage in her room with the door closed, Eli reading by flashlight (he thought she didn't know), Finn in his own bed (still holding, four nights now).

"You're quiet," James said.

"Thinking."

"About?"

Maeve pulled her knees up, wrapped her arms around them. "A student. Linda. She's having heart surgery in three weeks."

"Is she going to be okay?"

"They say it's routine. But she's terrified. She sat with me after class and just... cried."

James was quiet for a moment. "That must be hard. Holding space for that."

"It is." Maeve paused. "But it's also... I don't know. It's the job. It's the honor of the job. People come to yoga and they think it's about their hamstrings, but it's not. It's about their hearts. Their actual, literal hearts. And sometimes their hearts are breaking."

"Or failing."

"Or failing."

James reached over, took her hand. His fingers were warm, calloused from yard work, familiar as her own.

"You give a lot," he said. "To your students. To the kids. To me. But who holds space for you?"

"You do."

"Do I?"

The question hung in the air. Not accusatory. Just honest.

"I don't know," Maeve admitted. "I don't know if I let you. I don't know if I let anyone. I'm so used to being the one who holds that I don't know how to be held."

James squeezed her hand. "Maybe that's the practice."

"What is?"

"Learning to be held. Learning to let someone else carry the bucket for a while. Even if it's cracked. Even if it leaks."

Maeve smiled. He'd been listening. All these years, all these nights on the lanai when she'd talked through her themes, worked out what she wanted to say—he'd been listening.

"The Mustard Seed," she said. "That's what I taught today. About Kisa Gotami and the Buddha. How she went door to door looking for a house that had never known death, and every house had known it. Every single one."

"What's the lesson?"

"That we're not alone. That suffering is universal. That grief connects us instead of separating us."

"Do you believe that?"

Maeve thought about Linda, crying on her mat. About the woman in the story, carrying her dead son through the village. About every student who had ever walked into her studio carrying something invisible and heavy.

"I believe it for other people," she said. "I believe it when I'm teaching it. But when it's my turn to suffer? I forget. I think I'm the only one. I think no one could possibly understand."

"That's human."

"Is it?"

"Every house has known death, Maeve. Including ours. Including yours."

She leaned into him. Let her head rest on his shoulder. Let him carry her weight, just for a moment.

"I'm scared sometimes," she whispered.

"Of what?"

"That my heart will stop. That I'll miss something. That one of the kids will get sick and I won't be able to fix it. That you'll leave. That I'll wake up one day and realize I spent my whole life teaching other people how to live while forgetting to live myself."

James didn't answer right away. He just held her. Let her words exist without trying to fix them.

"Kisa Gotami," he finally said.

"What about her?"

"She thought she was alone. She wasn't. She thought her suffering was singular. It wasn't. She thought she needed medicine. What she needed was connection."

Maeve lifted her head. Looked at him.

"When did you get so wise?"

"I've been listening to you talk through your classes for fifteen years. Some of it sinks in."

She laughed. A real laugh, the kind that came from somewhere deep.

"I love you."

"I know." He kissed her forehead. "I love you too. Even your cracked bucket. Especially your cracked bucket."

They sat in the quiet, listening to the wind in the trees, the distant hum of traffic, the sleeping house behind them.

Tomorrow there would be more classes. More students with breaking hearts. More lessons she would teach and then have to learn herself.

But tonight, she wasn't alone.

Tonight, she was held.

She closed her eyes.

She slept.

11

The Monks and the Scorpion

It is the scorpion's nature to sting. It is my nature to save.

A monk was walking by a river when he saw a scorpion drowning.

Maeve stood at the front of the room, Tuesday evening, 6 p.m.—the after-work crowd, eighteen students still wearing the tension of their days. She'd taught this parable before, many times, but tonight it felt different. Heavier. Like the words were pressing against something she didn't want to look at.

"He reached into the water to save it," she said. "And the scorpion stung him."

She walked between the mats, her voice low and steady.

"He pulled his hand back, shook off the pain, and

reached in again. The scorpion stung him again. A student watching from the riverbank called out: 'Teacher! Why do you keep trying? Don't you see it will only sting you?'"

She paused at the front of the room.

"And the monk said: 'It is the scorpion's nature to sting. It is my nature to save. Why should I give up my nature because of his?'"

Maeve let the words settle.

"Tonight, I want you to think about your nature. The thing at your core that doesn't change, no matter how many times you get stung. And I want you to think about the scorpions in your life—the people who sting, not because they're evil, but because it's their nature. The question isn't whether they'll sting. They will. The question is: will you abandon your nature because of theirs?"

She brought her hands to her heart.

"Let's begin."

The class moved through a strong vinyasa flow. Maeve had needed the heat tonight, the physicality, the sweat. Something to burn through the knot in her chest that had been tightening all day.

She'd seen the Instagram post that morning.

Rae—her Rae, the teacher she'd trained five years ago, mentored, given her first classes, watched grow from a nervous newbie to a confident instructor—had posted a photo of an empty studio space. Bamboo floors. White walls. Big windows. The caption:

Coming soon: Sunrise Yoga Anchor Bay. A new space for our community to grow. DM for founding member rates!

Maeve had stared at the photo for a long time. Then she'd scrolled through the comments.

So excited for you! Finally! Can't wait! Will you have hot classes? I'm IN.

And then the one that made her stomach drop:

Rae told us about it in class last week! I already signed up!

Last week. Rae had been telling students—Maeve's students—about her new studio in Maeve's space. Before class. After class. In the parking lot. Inviting them to leave.

And she'd never said a word to Maeve.

Not a heads up. Not a thank you. Not even the courtesy of a conversation.

Maeve had found out through Instagram, like a stranger.

"Warrior two," she called, moving through the room. "Strong legs. Soft shoulders. Find your drishti."

She adjusted a student's back knee, offered a block to another. The mechanical tasks of teaching. The body on autopilot while the mind churned.

She'd trained Rae. Given her shifts when she was struggling financially. Covered her classes when her mother was sick. Written her a reference letter when she applied for a teaching certification. Treated her like family.

And Rae had been recruiting Maeve's students for weeks without saying a word.

"Reverse warrior," Maeve said. "Reach back. Open the heart."

The sting wasn't the competition. Maeve didn't own yoga in Anchor Bay. Other studios existed; more would open. That was fine. That was business.

The sting was the silence. The sneaking. The smile Rae had given her last Thursday—"Great class, Maeve!"—knowing she was about to open a competing studio and had already invited half the room.

"Triangle pose. Extend through the crown of your head."

It is the scorpion's nature to sting.

But did it have to be? Couldn't Rae have just... told her? Said, "Hey, I'm ready to do my own thing. Thank you for everything you've taught me. I hope there's no hard feelings"?

That's what Maeve would have done. That's what any decent person would have done.

But Rae wasn't Maeve. Rae was Rae. And apparently, Rae's nature was to take what she needed and slip out the back door.

"Come to standing. Shake it out."

After class, Maeve sat in her car in the parking lot. She didn't want to go home yet. Didn't want to explain the tightness in her jaw, the way her hands were shaking slightly on the steering wheel.

Her phone buzzed. James.

ETA?

20 min. Need to decompress.

Everything ok?

She stared at the question. Was everything okay? Her business was fine. Her marriage was good. Her kids were healthy. In the grand scheme of things, this was nothing. A minor betrayal. A small sting.

But it didn't feel small.

Rae's opening her own studio. Found out on Instagram.

Three dots. Then:

The one you trained?

Yep.

Did she tell you?

Nope. Been recruiting my students for weeks apparently.

A long pause. Then:

That's shitty.

Maeve almost laughed. James wasn't one for elaborate emotional processing. "That's shitty" was about as much as she'd get. But somehow, it was enough. Acknowledgment. Validation. Yes, this is shitty. You're not crazy for feeling hurt.

Coming home now.

She didn't sleep well that night. Kept replaying conversations, looking for signs she'd missed. Had Rae seemed distant lately? Had there been hints? Or had Maeve just been too busy, too trusting, too naive?

At 2 a.m., she gave up on sleep and went downstairs.

Made tea. Sat in the dark living room with her hands wrapped around the warm mug.

The scorpion story. She'd taught it that evening without realizing she was teaching it to herself.

It is the scorpion's nature to sting.

Was this Rae's nature? Looking back, Maeve could see it now. The way Rae had talked about other teachers—little digs disguised as observations. The way she'd positioned herself as the "cool" instructor, subtly differentiating herself from Maeve's "traditional" approach. The way she'd collected students' phone numbers, started a separate group text, built her own little kingdom within Maeve's space.

Maeve had noticed these things. She'd dismissed them. Given Rae the benefit of the doubt. Assumed good intentions.

It is my nature to save.

Was that Maeve's nature? To keep reaching in, keep getting stung, keep believing the scorpion would change?

She thought about other times she'd been stung. Friends who'd taken without giving. Family members who'd crossed boundaries. Students who'd complained publicly after she'd bent over backward for them privately.

Every time, she'd reached back in. Given another chance. Assumed the best.

And every time, eventually, the sting.

But the monk in the story didn't stop reaching. That

was the point. He didn't abandon his nature just because the scorpion couldn't abandon its own.

So what was Maeve supposed to do? Keep reaching? Or finally, finally, let the damn scorpion drown?

The next morning, she taught her 6 a.m. class. Then her 9 a.m. Linda was there—she'd come back, as promised, before her Paris trip. Maeve gave her an extra long hug after class.

"I'm going," Linda said. "Paris. We leave Friday."

"Good. Taste the strawberry."

"I will. Thank you. For everything."

Maeve watched her go, feeling the familiar mix of love and fear. Would she see Linda again? Would the surgery go well? Would the strawberry be worth the risk?

She didn't know. She couldn't know. She could only show up, teach the lesson, and trust.

At 10:30, between classes, she sat in her office and stared at her phone. R'aes Instagram post. 847 likes now. Comments still rolling in.

She could post something. A passive-aggressive response. A "support local yoga" message. A not-so-subtle dig.

She could call Rae out. Send a text. Demand an explanation. Make her feel as small as Maeve felt.

She could badmouth her to students. Drop hints. Let people know what Rae had done.

These options felt satisfying in theory. Righteous. Justified.

But they weren't her nature.

Her nature was to teach. To show up. To keep the door open, even when people walked out of it. To trust that what she'd built in fifteen years couldn't be stolen by someone else's Instagram post.

It is the scorpion's nature to sting. It is my nature to save.

She didn't have to save Rae. That wasn't the point. The point was that she didn't have to become a scorpion herself. She didn't have to sting back.

She could just... let it go.

Not forgive—that felt like too much to ask right now. Not forget—she'd remember this. But let it go. Stop reaching into that particular river. Let the scorpion swim away.

She closed Instagram. Opened her class planning document. Started working on next week's sequence.

The studio was still here. The students who wanted to stay would stay. The ones who left would leave. That had always been true. It would always be true.

She could only control her own nature.

That night, James found her on the lanai again, knees pulled up, staring at the stars.

"How you doing?" he asked, settling into the chair beside her.

"Better. I think."

"Did you talk to her?"

"Rae? No."

"Are you going to?"

Maeve considered the question. "I don't think so. What would be the point? She knows what she did. If she wanted to have a conversation, she would have had one before she did it."

"That's mature of you."

"Or avoidant."

James shrugged. "Sometimes mature and avoidant look the same from the outside."

Maeve laughed. "Wow. Profound."

"I'm full of wisdom. It's all the secondhand yoga I've absorbed."

She leaned her head back, looked at the sky. "The thing that gets me... I've seen her do this to other people. Talk behind their backs. Take what she needed and move on. I just thought—"

"That you were different."

"Yeah. That she wouldn't do it to me. Because I'd been good to her. Because we were friends."

"But you weren't different."

"No." Maeve felt the sting of that truth. "I wasn't."

"Some people just take. It's not personal. It's just who they are."

They sat in comfortable silence for a while. The winds rustled through the palms. Somewhere down the street, a dog barked.

"I taught this story tonight," Maeve finally said. "About a monk and a scorpion. The monk keeps reaching into the water to save the scorpion, and the scorpion keeps stinging him. A student asks why he bothers, and the monk says, 'It's the scorpion's nature to sting. It's my nature to save. Why should I give up my nature because of his?'"

James considered this. "So Rae's the scorpion."

"I guess. But the monk in the story doesn't stop reaching in. He keeps trying. And I don't know if that's wise or just... stupid."

"Maybe neither." James shifted in his chair. "Maybe the point isn't whether you keep reaching. Maybe it's just knowing who you're dealing with. So when they sting, you're not surprised. You don't take it personally. You just think, 'Right. Scorpion.'"

Maeve turned to look at him. "When did you get so smart?"

"I've always been smart. You were just too busy doing chaturangas to notice."

She reached over, took his hand.

"I don't want to become bitter," she said. "I don't want to start seeing scorpions everywhere. Assuming the worst. Closing myself off."

"You won't."

"How do you know?"

"Because it's not your nature." He squeezed her hand. "You'll get stung again. Probably more than once. But you'll keep being you. Open. Generous. Trusting. That's not weakness. That's just... Maeve."

She felt tears prick her eyes. Not from sadness—from being seen. From being known.

"What if I lose students? What if her studio is better? What if—"

"Then you'll figure it out. You always do."

"What if I don't?"

"Then I'll still be here. The kids will still be here. The things that actually matter will still be here."

Maeve leaned into him. Let her head rest on his shoulder. Let the knot in her chest loosen, just slightly.

Rae was going to open her studio. Some students would leave. That was reality.

But Maeve was still Maeve. Her nature hadn't changed. Her heart hadn't hardened.

The scorpion would sting. That was inevitable.

But the monk could still be the monk.

She closed her eyes.

She slept.

12

Maybe, Maybe Not
Good luck, bad luck—who knows?

There was a farmer whose horse ran away.

Maeve stood at the front of the room, Thursday morning, 9 a.m.—her favorite class, the one that drew the regulars, the ones who'd been coming for years. Sixteen students on their mats, faces she knew by heart.

"His neighbors came to console him," she said. "'Such bad luck!' they cried. And the farmer just shrugged and said, 'Maybe.'"

She walked between the mats, but slower than usual. Careful.

"The next day, the horse returned—and brought three wild horses with it. The neighbors came back, excited this time. 'Such good luck!' And the farmer said, 'Maybe.'"

She returned to the front, cradling her left wrist against her body without thinking about it.

"The farmer's son tried to tame one of the wild horses and was thrown off. He broke his leg. The neighbors shook their heads. 'Such bad luck!' The farmer said, 'Maybe.' A week later, the army came through the village, conscripting all the young men for war. But the son, with his broken leg, was spared. The neighbors marveled. 'Such good luck!' And the farmer—"

"Said maybe," a student in the front row finished, smiling.

"Said maybe." Maeve smiled back. "We never know what anything means until we know. And sometimes we never know. The horse runs away—is that bad? The son breaks his leg—is that bad? We rush to judge every moment, but the farmer teaches us to pause. To wait. To trust that the story isn't finished yet."

She brought her hands together at her heart—then winced.

"Today, I want you to practice 'maybe.' When something feels hard, instead of labeling it bad, just notice. Maybe. When something feels good, instead of clinging to it, just notice. Maybe. Let the story unfold without deciding what it means."

She took a breath.

"I should tell you—I hurt my wrist this week. Domestic incident involving a five-year-old and a phone." A few sympathetic laughs. "So today, I'm going to teach a little differently. I won't be demonstrating everything. You'll have to listen to my words instead of watching my body. Maybe that's bad luck. Or maybe..."

"Maybe," the class echoed.

"Let's begin."

It had happened Sunday afternoon.

She'd been bent over picking something up off the floor—she couldn't even remember what now, which was the thing about motherhood, there was always something on the floor, always something to pick up, always some task half-finished while another one started.

Finn had her phone. Why did he have her phone? She couldn't remember that either. Maybe she'd handed it to him to buy herself thirty seconds. Maybe he'd grabbed it off the counter. The details were lost in the blur of a Sunday with three kids.

What she did remember was the sound. A dull thunk. And then pain—sharp, electric, wrong—blooming across her wrist.

"Ow!" She'd yelped, clutching her arm to her chest. "Finn, what—"

He was already crying. "I didn't mean to! It slipped!"

The phone had dropped directly onto her wrist. The edge of it, the corner, landing on the exact spot where bone met tendon. A one-in-a-million shot. The kind of thing that shouldn't hurt as much as it did.

"It's okay, buddy, it's okay—" She was comforting

him even as the pain radiated up her arm, even as she knew something was wrong. Because that's what you did. You yelped, and then you let it go, because there was too much happening, because someone was always crying, because dinner needed to be made and homework needed to be checked and the dog needed to go out.

She'd pushed through the rest of the day. Iced it when she remembered. Told herself it would be fine by morning.

It wasn't fine by morning.

The urgent care doctor had been kind but direct. "It's not broken, but it's its inflamed might be some tissue damage. You need to rest it. No weight-bearing for at least three weeks. Ideally six."

"I'm a yoga teacher."

"Then you'll need to modify."

Modify. Such a small word for such a massive shift.

The first few days had been brutal.

Maeve hadn't realized how much of her teaching lived in her body until her body wouldn't cooperate. She'd reach for a demonstration and pain would stop her. She'd start to flow and have to catch herself. Every chaturanga, every downward dog, every plank—impossible.

She'd taught Monday's class in a fog of frustration. Talked too much. Overexplained. Watched her students struggle to follow verbal cues they'd never needed before because they'd always just watched her.

"That was rough," James had said when she got home, reading her face.

"I don't know how to teach without my body."

"You'll figure it out."

"What if I don't? What if this is it? What if I've been relying on demonstration so much that I actually can't teach without it?"

James had just looked at her. Patient. Waiting.

"Maybe," he'd finally said.

She'd thrown a pillow at him.

But Thursday was different.

Thursday, something shifted.

"Warrior one," Maeve said, standing at the front of the room with her hands at her heart instead of raised overhead. "Front knee bends toward ninety degrees—but don't look down to check. Feel it. Is your knee tracking over your ankle? Can you sense the stretch through your back hip flexor?"

She watched her students. Really watched, without the distraction of her own body moving.

"Jennifer, see if you can soften your shoulders away from your ears. David, your back foot is turning in—try to keep the outer edge pressing down."

She was seeing things she'd never seen before. Details she'd missed when she was busy demonstrating. The way Tom always held tension in his jaw. The way Maria's left hip was tighter than her right. The way Sarah rushed through transitions like she was trying to get somewhere.

"Warrior two. Open your hips to the side wall. Feel the opposition—front knee pressing forward, back leg pressing back. Like you're being pulled in two directions at once."

She walked between the mats, adjusting with her right hand, offering verbal cues instead of physical assists.

"That's it. Breathe into the space you're creating. You don't have to go anywhere. You're already there."

By the end of class, something had changed. The room felt different. Quieter. More focused. Students were listening in a way they hadn't before—because they had to. Because Maeve's words were all they had.

"Savasana," she said. "Let your body be heavy. Let the floor hold you. You worked hard today. Now rest."

She sat at the front of the room, watching them settle. Her wrist throbbed dully, but distantly now. Background noise.

Maybe this was bad luck. A stupid fall, a sprained wrist, weeks of modification.

Or maybe.

After class, Maria lingered.

"That was amazing," she said. "I don't know what was different, but I felt like I actually understood the poses today. Like, in my body. Not just copying what you were doing."

Maeve smiled. "Really?"

"Yeah. Usually I'm so focused on watching you that I'm not really paying attention to myself. Today I had to. And it was..." She paused, searching for the word. "Deeper. Is that weird?"

"It's not weird."

"Are you going to teach like this from now on? Even when your wrist heals?"

Maeve hadn't thought that far ahead. "Maybe."

Maria laughed. "That's the lesson, isn't it? Maybe."

That night, Maeve sat on the lanai with an ice pack on her wrist. The kids were inside—Sage doing homework, Eli reading, Finn building something elaborate with Legos that would inevitably end up underfoot at 2 a.m.

James brought her tea without being asked. Sat down beside her.

"How was class?"

"Good. Actually good." She adjusted the ice pack. "Something Maria said got me thinking. She said she understood the poses better today because she couldn't watch me. She had to feel them herself."

"Makes sense."

"But I've been teaching for fifteen years with my body. Demonstrating everything. What if that was actually... getting in the way?"

James considered this. "You know how Finn learned to ride his bike?"

"By falling off it repeatedly?"

"By me letting go." He took a sip of his tea. "I used to hold the back of his seat the whole time. Keep him steady. But he never really learned until I let go and let him wobble. Let him feel what balance actually was instead of relying on me to provide it."

Maeve looked at him. "When did you become a philosopher?"

"I've always been a philosopher. You just never asked."

She leaned into him, careful with her wrist. "So you're saying my injury is like letting go of Finn's bike seat."

"I'm saying maybe it is. Or maybe it's just a sprained wrist and you're overthinking it. But either way—" he shrugged— "maybe."

She laughed. Actually laughed, for the first time since Sunday.

"I hate that word now."

"No you don't. You love it. It's the most yogic word there is. Complete non-attachment to outcomes."

"Since when do you know what's yogic?"

"Since I married a yoga teacher and have spent fifteen years absorbing wisdom through osmosis."

Over the next two weeks, Maeve experimented.

She taught some classes from her mat, moving through modifications while the students did full expressions. She taught other classes standing still, using only her voice. She taught one class—an experiment—with her eyes closed, guiding purely by sound and presence.

That one was a disaster. Three students bumped into each other, someone knocked over a water bottle, and Maeve walked straight into the props shelf. But they'd all laughed about it afterward, and someone said it was the most memorable class they'd ever taken.

The students adapted. Some preferred the new style—the verbal cues, the deeper listening. Others missed the visual guidance and asked when she'd be back to "normal."

"I don't know," Maeve told them. "Maybe never. Maybe next week. We'll see."

The uncertainty that would have terrified her a month ago now felt almost comfortable. Like a loose garment instead of a straitjacket.

Three weeks after the injury, Maeve went back to the doctor.

"It's healing well," the doctor said, rotating her wrist gently. "You can start putting some weight on it. Slowly. Listen to your body."

"Can I do a chaturanga?"

"Not yet. Maybe in another two weeks. And even then, modify. Don't push it."

Maeve nodded. Two more weeks of teaching without her full body. Two more weeks of learning whatever this was teaching her.

Maybe that was bad luck.

Or maybe it was exactly what she needed. A forced pause. A chance to discover that she was more than her demonstrations. That her voice was enough. That her students could find their own way if she stopped showing them hers.

The farmer's horse had run away. His son had broken his leg. The army had come and gone.

And through it all, the farmer just kept saying: maybe.

That night, after the kids were in bed, Maeve tried a sun salutation for the first time since the injury. Slowly. Carefully. Modified chaturanga—knees down, chest barely grazing the floor.

Her wrist complained but didn't scream.

She moved through the sequence again. And again. Feeling her body wake up to itself, tentative and grateful.

James watched from the doorway.

"How does it feel?"

"Different. Weaker. But also..." She paused in downward dog, head hanging between her arms. "I'm paying attention in a way I haven't in years. Every movement matters. I can't just autopilot through it."

"Beginner's mind."

"Something like that."

She came to standing, rolled out her neck, smiled at him.

"You know what? I think I'm actually grateful. For the injury. For all of it."

"Careful. That sounds like you're assigning meaning."

"You're right." She walked over, kissed him on the cheek. "Maybe I'm grateful. Or maybe I'm just tired and slightly delirious."

"Maybe."

"Stop saying maybe."

"Never."

She pushed past him into the house, but she was laughing. And her wrist was healing. And her teaching was changing. And the story wasn't finished yet.

Linda texted the next morning.

Made it back from Paris. Surgery is Tuesday. Scared but ready. Thank you for everything.

Maeve typed back: *You've got this. I'll be thinking of you. Maybe send me a photo of the Eiffel Tower?*

A minute later, a photo arrived. Linda in front of the tower, her daughter beside her, both of them grinning like they'd gotten away with something.

Best strawberry I ever tasted, Linda wrote.

Maeve smiled at her phone. Set it down. Went to teach her 9 a.m. class.

Modified. Verbal. Different.

Maybe better. Maybe just different.

Either way—maybe.

13

Chapter Thirteen
The Moon Cannot Be Stolen

Poor fellow. I wish I could have given him this beautiful moon.

Ryokan was a Zen master who lived simply in a small hut at the foot of a mountain.

Maeve stood at the front of the room, Saturday morning, 9 a.m.—and the room was full. Fuller than usual. Because it was December, and the seasonal yogis had returned.

"One evening, a thief visited his hut," Maeve said, her voice soft in the heated space. "But he found nothing to steal. Ryokan lived with almost nothing—a mat, a bowl, his robes."

She looked around the room at the familiar faces. Barbara and Stan from Minnesota, here for six weeks to escape the cold. The Hendersons from Chicago, visiting their daughter who'd moved to Anchor Bay three years ago. Michael, who spent half the year in Seattle and half here, following the sun. Faces she only saw in winter, faces that felt like family walking through the door.

"When Ryokan returned and found the thief, he didn't call for help. He didn't get angry. He said: 'You've come a long way to visit me. You shouldn't leave empty-handed. Please—take my clothes as a gift.'"

She walked between the mats, stepping carefully around the extra bodies.

"The thief was bewildered. He took the clothes and left. And Ryokan sat naked in his hut, gazing out at the night sky. 'Poor fellow,' he said. 'I wish I could have given him this beautiful moon.'"

Maeve returned to the front, her hand drifting unconsciously to her heart.

"The thief thought wealth was in possessions. Ryokan knew that true wealth can't be stolen. The moon, the stars, the peace in his own heart—these were his riches. No one could take them."

She paused, feeling the weight of the words differently today.

"This week, I want you to think about what can't be stolen from you. What you carry that doesn't depend on circumstances. The love you've given. The moments you've fully lived. The people who've shaped you. These are your moons. No thief can reach them."

Her voice caught slightly. She steadied herself.

"Let's begin."

. . .

The seasonal yogis.

Maeve loved them in a particular way—different from the regulars who came every week, different from the drop-ins who appeared and disappeared. The seasonals were like migratory birds. They arrived with the winter, filled the room with their presence, and then —just when she'd gotten used to them—they flew away again.

Barbara had been coming for eleven years. She always set up in the same spot, second row left, and she always brought Stan even though Stan clearly would rather be golfing. But he came, because Barbara came, and after class he always said the same thing: "Well, that was something."

The Hendersons—Tom and Ruth—had started coming five years ago when their daughter Sarah had her first baby. Now they came every December and every March, and Maeve had watched their grandchildren grow from infants to toddlers to actual small people through the photos Ruth showed her after class.

Michael was a different kind of seasonal. He wasn't visiting anyone—he was just following the weather, the way some people followed the sun. He'd sold his accounting practice eight years ago, bought a condo here and a condo in Seattle, and spent his life in permanent migration. "I'm like a whale," he'd told Maeve once. "But with better real estate."

When they walked in this morning—Barbara first,

then the Hendersons, then Michael—Maeve had felt something loosen in her chest. Like seeing family at the airport. Like proof that the world still worked the way it was supposed to.

"You look good," Barbara had said, hugging her before class. "Tired, but good."

"I am tired. But it's the good kind."

"Is there a good kind?"

"There must be. I keep telling myself there is."

Barbara had laughed and gone to her spot, second row left, where Stan was already unrolling her mat for her the wrong way, the way he always did, the way Barbara always fixed without comment.

These rituals. These returns. These people who appeared and disappeared and appeared again, like the tide.

Maeve had taught the class with a full heart. The room was crowded—twenty-three bodies instead of the usual fourteen—and the energy was different. Louder. More chaotic. More alive.

She'd missed this. She hadn't known how much until they walked through the door.

After class, Maeve checked her phone. Three missed calls from a number she didn't recognize, and a voicemail.

She stepped into her office, closed the door, pressed play.

"Hello, this message is for Maeve Campbell. This is Patricia Chen from Coastal Property Management. I'm calling about the building at 847 Main Street. I'm afraid I have some difficult news. Please call me back at your earliest convenience."

Maeve stared at the phone. 847 Main Street. The studio.

She called back.

"Ms. Campbell, thank you for returning my call. I'm sorry to have to tell you this over the phone, but Eleanor Matsuda passed away on Thursday."

The room tilted.

Eleanor. Her landlord. The woman who'd taken a chance on her fifteen years ago when she was nobody—just a yoga teacher with a dream and not enough money. Eleanor had looked at her across the desk and said, "I believe in you. Pay me what you can until you can pay me more."

"Ms. Campbell? Are you there?"

"Yes. I'm—yes. I'm here." Maeve sat down heavily in her chair. "What happened?"

"She passed peacefully in her sleep. She was ninety-one."

Ninety-one. Maeve had known Eleanor was old, but somehow she'd stopped seeing her age. Eleanor had just been Eleanor—sharp, funny, always wearing those bright scarves, always asking about the kids.

"I'm calling because there will be some changes to the property management," Patricia continued. "Eleanor's estate is being handled by her nephew, David Matsuda. He'll be reaching out to all tenants in the coming weeks to discuss the transition."

"Transition?"

"I don't have details yet. But I wanted you to hear about Eleanor from us rather than finding out another way."

After she hung up, Maeve sat in the silence of her office. The muffled sounds of students chatting in the lobby filtered through the door. Someone laughed. A mat bag zipped.

Eleanor was gone.

Fifteen years ago, Maeve had walked into Eleanor's office with a business plan she'd printed at Kinko's and a desperate hope. She'd been twenty-eight, newly certified, teaching out of gyms and church basements, dreaming of something more.

Eleanor had listened to her entire pitch without interrupting. Then she'd looked at Maeve over her reading glasses and said: "You know this space has been empty for two years? Everyone who's looked at it wants to turn it into a restaurant or a nail salon. But I don't want a restaurant. I want something that makes people feel better when they leave than when they came in."

"That's what yoga does," Maeve had said.

"I know. That's why I'm saying yes."

The first year had been brutal. Maeve had taught eighteen classes a week, cleaned the studio herself, survived on protein bars and anxiety. There were months she couldn't make the full rent. Eleanor had never once threatened to evict her. She'd just said, "Pay me when you can. I'm not going anywhere."

When the pandemic hit and Maeve had to close for

two years, Eleanor had called her personally. "Don't worry about the rent. Just survive. The space will be here when you're ready."

She'd reduced Maeve's rent to almost nothing for those two years. Refused to take a penny more than Maeve could afford. "I'm ninety-one years old," she'd said. "What do I need the money for? I'd rather have you here when this is over."

And Maeve had survived. And the space had been here. And Eleanor had been at the reopening, wearing one of her bright scarves, drinking the cheap champagne, telling everyone who would listen that she'd known from the beginning this one was special.

That was eighteen months ago. The last time Maeve had seen her.

She should have visited more. Should have called. Should have brought the kids by like she'd always meant to. But there was always something—a class to teach, a kid to pick up, a crisis to manage. The visit she kept planning to make, the thank-you she kept meaning to say.

Now Eleanor was gone. And the things Maeve hadn't said couldn't be said.

She taught her afternoon class in a fog. Went through the motions—the cues, the adjustments, the gentle corrections—but her mind was somewhere else. With Eleanor. With the building. With the nephew she'd never met who would now decide the future of the space she'd built her life in.

After class, Barbara lingered.

"You okay? You seem far away today."

"My landlord died. Eleanor. She—" Maeve stopped, surprised by the tears that suddenly pressed behind her eyes. "She believed in me when no one else did. Fifteen years ago. She gave me this space."

Barbara didn't say anything. She just opened her arms.

Maeve let herself be held. Just for a moment. Let the grief surface, let the tears come, let someone else carry her weight.

"She sounds like a moon," Barbara said quietly.

Maeve pulled back, wiped her face. "What?"

"The story you told this morning. The Zen master and the thief. The things that can't be stolen. Eleanor sounds like one of your moons."

Maeve considered this. The love Eleanor had given her. The belief. The chance. No one could take those away. They lived in her, in the studio, in every class she taught.

"She was," Maeve said. "She really was."

That night, Maeve sat on the lanai alone. James had taken the kids out for pizza—she'd asked for the quiet, needed it, and he'd understood without her having to explain.

She thought about Eleanor. About the seasonal yogis who had returned. About the things that came and went and came again, and the things that came and went and didn't come back.

The seasonals would leave in a few weeks. Barbara would return to Minnesota, the Hendersons to Chicago, Michael to Seattle. The room would get smaller again, quieter, back to its winter self.

But they'd return next year. That was the deal. That was the rhythm.

Eleanor wouldn't return. That was a different kind of leaving.

But the moon—Eleanor's belief, her generosity, her scarves and her sharp wit—that couldn't be stolen. It lived in the studio now. In Maeve. In every student who walked through the door of the space Eleanor had entrusted to her.

"Poor fellow," Ryokan had said, watching the thief disappear. "I wish I could have given him this beautiful moon."

Eleanor had given Maeve her moon. Fifteen years of it. And now it was Maeve's to keep.

Her phone buzzed. A text from James:
Kids are fed. Bringing home ice cream. You okay?
She smiled.
I'm okay. Sad, but okay.
That's allowed.
I know. It's just—she was one of the good ones.
The good ones leave the biggest holes.

Maeve looked up at the sky. Clear tonight, the stars bright, the moon nearly full.

Eleanor had believed in her before she'd earned it.

Had given her space to grow into herself. Had refused to let money or convenience trump faith in a person.

That was wealth that couldn't be counted. That was a moon no thief could steal.

Tomorrow there would be phone calls. The nephew. The estate. The uncertainty of what came next for the building, the lease, the studio she'd built from nothing.

But tonight, she could just sit with the loss. Let it be what it was. Honor the woman who'd made everything possible.

The seasonal yogis would leave and return. That was their rhythm.

Eleanor had left and wouldn't return. That was grief.

But the moon remained. The moon always remained.

Maeve closed her eyes.

She let herself remember.

14

Set It Down

I left her at the river. Why are you still carrying her?

Two monks were traveling together when they came to a river with a strong current.

Maeve stood at the front of the room, Wednesday evening, 6 p.m.—the after-work class, twelve students arranged on their mats. Her voice was steady, but something beneath it wasn't.

"A young woman was standing at the edge, unable to cross. Without a word, the elder monk picked her up, carried her across the water, and set her down on the other side. Then he continued walking."

She moved between the mats slowly.

"The younger monk was shocked. They had taken vows not to touch women. He followed in silence, but his mind was churning. Hours passed. Finally, he couldn't contain himself. 'How could you carry that woman? We're not supposed to touch women! It's against our vows!'"

Maeve returned to the front.

"The elder monk looked at him calmly and said: 'I set her down at the river. Why are you still carrying her?'"

She let the silence hold.

"We do this. We pick things up—a comment someone made, a slight, a rejection, a confusion—and we carry them for hours. Days. Years. Long after the moment has passed, we're still holding it. Still turning it over. Still asking why."

Her throat tightened. She pushed through.

"Today, I want you to notice what you're still carrying. What river did you cross days or weeks ago that you haven't set down yet? What are you holding that's only heavy because you won't let it go?"

She brought her hands to her heart.

"Let's begin."

The text had come three days ago.

Maeve had been making dinner—pasta, the easy kind, the kind you make when you're tired and no one will eat anything complicated anyway—when her phone buzzed.

I think it's best if we take some space. I wish you well.

She'd stared at it, sauce-covered spoon suspended over the pot.

It was from Jenna.

Jenna, who she'd known for ten years. Jenna, who came for private sessions every Tuesday at 4 p.m.—had come, past tense now. Jenna, who she'd grandfathered in at a lower rate because she'd been one of Maeve's first private students, back when Maeve was charging practically nothing just to build a client base.

Jenna, who told her everything. The divorce. The dating disasters. The estranged sister. The mother who called too much and said too little. Ten years of stories, of laughter, of the particular intimacy that forms when you see someone's body struggle through poses week after week and never judge.

I think it's best if we take some space.

Maeve had typed back immediately: *Is everything okay? Did I do something?*

No response.

She'd waited an hour. Tried again: *I'm confused. Can we talk about this?*

Nothing.

The pasta had burned. Sage had complained. Finn had cried about something unrelated. Eli had asked why she was being weird. Maeve had smiled and said she wasn't, everything was fine, who wants garlic bread?

But she'd checked her phone eleven times before bed.

No response.

The next day, she'd called. Straight to voicemail.

She'd texted again: *Jenna, I really don't understand*

what happened. Ten years of friendship deserves at least a conversation. Please.

Read. No reply.

That was when Maeve started replaying everything. The last session—had she said something wrong? Been distracted? Jenna had seemed fine, laughing about her latest Hinge disaster, complaining about her boss. Normal. Completely normal.

The session before that. The one before that. Nothing. No warning signs. No tension. Just Tuesday at 4 p.m., same as always, and then—gone.

She'd started asking questions she couldn't answer. Was it something she'd said weeks ago that Jenna had been holding onto? Was it something she didn't say? Had she failed to show up in some way she couldn't see?

The not-knowing was the worst part. If Jenna had said, "You did this thing and it hurt me," Maeve could have apologized. Could have understood. Could have tried to fix it.

But there was nothing to fix. Just silence where a decade of friendship used to be.

"Warrior two," Maeve called, watching her students shift into the pose. "Strong legs. Soft face. Find your drishti."

She adjusted a student's back foot. Offered a block to another.

The thing about Jenna was—Maeve had seen her do this before.

Over the years, Jenna had cut people off. A college

friend who'd "betrayed" her in some vague way Jenna never fully explained. A coworker who'd "crossed a line." A woman from a book club who'd "shown her true colors."

Jenna had told Maeve these stories, and Maeve had listened. Had nodded sympathetically. Had assumed, without examining the assumption, that these people must have done something to deserve it.

She'd never considered that one day, she'd be one of them.

"Reverse warrior. Reach back. Open the side body."

There had been others at the studio, too. Women Jenna had been close to, then suddenly wasn't. Maeve had noticed the pattern but hadn't named it. Hadn't wanted to see it, maybe. Because Jenna was her friend. Because they were different.

Except they weren't different.

Jenna had a trapdoor. You could get close—but only so close. The moment you crossed some invisible line, the moment you got too near to whatever she was protecting, the floor dropped out. You fell through, and she walked away.

Maeve had thought she was immune. Ten years. Surely that counted for something.

It didn't.

"Triangle pose," Maeve said. "Extend through the crown of your head."

She walked the room, making adjustments, but her mind was still at the river.

The worst part wasn't the loss. It was the confusion.

If Jenna had been angry, Maeve could have understood. If she'd said, "You hurt me," Maeve could have apologized. If she'd said, "I'm going through something and need distance," Maeve could have given her space with love.

But this—this clean severance, this surgical removal of a decade—she couldn't make sense of it.

I think it's best if we take some space. I wish you well.

Fourteen words. That's what ten years was worth. Fourteen words and a wall of silence.

"Come to standing. Close your eyes. Notice what you're holding."

Maeve closed her own eyes. Noticed what she was holding.

Jenna. She was still carrying Jenna. Still turning the text over in her mind. Still asking why. Still checking her phone like a response might magically appear.

I set her down at the river. Why are you still carrying her?

Because she didn't understand. Because it didn't make sense. Because her brain needed a reason, and there wasn't one—or if there was, she'd never know it.

Jenna was elusive. She always had been. You couldn't quite catch her, couldn't quite know her, couldn't quite pin down what was beneath the stories and the laughter and the Tuesday sessions. Some people said there was a lot under the surface. But Jenna never let anyone close enough to see it. And when you got too close—this happened.

"Let's take savasana," Maeve said. "Lie down. Let it all go."

After class, Maeve sat in her car in the parking lot. The familiar ritual of decompression. The moment between teacher and mother, between holding space and needing space.

She pulled out her phone. No new messages.

She typed: *I accept that you need space. I just want you to know that I care about you, and if you ever want to talk, I'm here.*

She stared at the words. Then she deleted them.

What was the point? Jenna had made her choice. Another message would just be Maeve carrying her further, refusing to set her down.

She thought about what James would say. Probably something simple and true. "Some people leave. It's not always about you."

She thought about what she'd tell a student going through this. "You can't make someone stay. You can only decide how long you carry them after they've gone."

She thought about the monk at the river. How he'd picked up the woman, carried her across, and set her down. No attachment. No story about what it meant. Just the action, and then the release.

Maeve couldn't do that yet. The wound was too fresh. The confusion too thick.

But she could start. She could notice that she was carrying Jenna. She could feel the weight of it. And she could choose, moment by moment, to loosen her grip.

She started the car. Drove home.

That night, James found her on the lanai. The usual spot. The usual quiet.

"You want to talk about it?"

"How do you know there's something to talk about?"

"Because you've checked your phone fourteen times since dinner and you're doing that thing with your jaw."

Maeve touched her jaw. Realized it was clenched. Let it go.

"Jenna ended our friendship. By text. Three days ago."

"The Tuesday private?"

"Ten years. Ten years of sessions and conversations and—" She stopped. "She just... ended it. No explanation. Won't respond to anything."

James was quiet for a moment. "That's brutal."

"It doesn't make sense. We were fine. We were completely fine. And then just—'I think it's best if we take some space.'"

"What do you think happened?"

"I have no idea. That's the thing. I've replayed everything. Every session, every conversation. There's nothing. No warning. Just—" She made a cutting motion with her hand. "Gone."

"Maybe it's not about you."

"Then why does it feel so personal?"

"Because it's personal to you. Doesn't mean it's about you."

Maeve considered this. She'd spent three days assuming she'd done something wrong. Looking for the mistake. Trying to find the thing she could fix.

But what if there was nothing to fix? What if Jenna just... did this? What if it was her pattern, her protection, her way of keeping everyone at arm's length by periodically burning the bridges?

"She's done this before," Maeve said slowly. "Cut people off. I always assumed they'd done something to deserve it."

"And now?"

"Now I think maybe that's just... who she is. How she survives. Get close, then disappear before anyone can really see you."

"That's sad."

"It is." Maeve felt something shift. Not forgiveness—not yet. But something softer. Understanding, maybe. Or the beginning of it. "She told me once that everyone leaves eventually. I thought she meant other people. Maybe she meant herself."

They sat in silence for a while. The trade winds rustled the palms. A car passed on the street below.

"I taught the two monks story tonight," Maeve said. "About setting things down at the river."

"Are you going to take your own advice?"

"Eventually. Not yet. But eventually."

"That's honest."

"It's all I've got."

James reached over, took her hand. "For what it's worth, I think the problem is hers, not yours. You don't cut off people who've been good to you for ten years unless something inside you is broken."

"Maybe. Or maybe I did something I can't see."

"Maybe. But you're not going to find out by carrying her around asking."

Maeve looked at the sky. The moon was waning now, just a sliver. In a few days, it would be dark entirely.

"I keep wanting to send one more text. Just to... I don't know. Keep the door open."

"What would it change?"

"Nothing, probably. But I'd know I tried."

"You already tried. You sent messages. You called. She knows the door is open. She's choosing not to walk through it."

Maeve nodded. He was right. She knew he was right.

But knowing and feeling were different countries. And she wasn't ready to cross the border yet.

She checked her phone one more time before bed. Still nothing.

She typed: *I'm letting this go now. I hope you find whatever you're looking for.*

She stared at the words.

Then she deleted them.

Jenna didn't need her closure. Jenna had already

closed the door herself, quietly, completely, without looking back.

Maeve was the one still standing at the river, holding something that wasn't hers to carry anymore.

She set down the phone. Turned off the light.

Tomorrow she'd probably pick Jenna up again. Turn her over. Ask why. That was okay. That was human. Grief didn't move in straight lines.

But tonight, just for tonight, she could practice setting her down.

She closed her eyes.

She tried to let go.

15

Chapter Fifteen
The Fish in the Ocean

You're swimming in it. It's everywhere—around you, inside you. It's what you're made of.

A young fish swam up to an older fish and asked: "I keep hearing about this thing called 'ocean.' Where is it?"

Maeve stood at the front of the room, Friday morning, 9 a.m.—her favorite class, the seekers, the ones who came for meaning as much as movement. Fifteen students on their mats.

"The older fish laughed and said: 'You're swimming in it. It's everywhere—around you, inside you. It's what you're made of.' But the young fish just swam away, still searching for the ocean."

She walked between the mats, her phone a familiar

weight in her pocket. She'd checked it three times before class. Force of habit. Addiction, maybe.

"We do this constantly. We search for peace while swimming in it. We look for enough while surrounded by abundance. We scroll through images of other people's lives, looking for something we already have."

She returned to the front, feeling the irony of her own words.

"Today, I want you to stop searching. Stop looking out there for what's already in here. The ocean isn't somewhere else. You're soaking in it."

She brought her hands to her heart.

"Let's begin."

The Instagram post had taken her forty-five minutes.

Forty-five minutes to write three sentences, choose a photo, find music that wasn't embarrassing, and add the right hashtags. Forty-five minutes she didn't have, carved out of the space between school drop-off and her first class.

And for what? Sixty-two likes. Four comments—two from bots, one from her mother, one from a student who came every week anyway.

This was her life now. Content creator. Social media manager. Canva designer. Reel producer. Hashtag researcher. Algorithm chaser.

When she'd opened the studio fifteen years ago, marketing meant a flyer at the coffee shop and word of mouth. Now it meant daily posts, stories that disappeared in twenty-four hours, reels that required music and transitions and text overlays, an endless feed of other studios doing it better, slicker, more viral.

She'd learned Canva. Watched YouTube tutorials on how to make reels. Downloaded apps that promised to optimize her posting schedule. Spent hours she didn't have trying to crack a code that kept changing.

And still, the other studios were growing faster. Still, her follower count plateaued. Still, she watched twenty-three-year-olds with ring lights and perfect abs build audiences in months that had taken her years.

You're swimming in it, she'd taught this morning. *Stop searching.*

But how do you stop searching when the search is your job?

"Mom, that song is so cringe."

Sage was leaning over Maeve's shoulder, watching her try to add music to a reel. A fifteen-second video of the studio at sunset, golden light through the windows, empty mats waiting.

"What's wrong with it?"

"It's just... no one uses that song anymore. It's giving 2022."

"What does that even mean?"

Sage sighed the sigh of a teenager burdened by a parent's digital incompetence. "Here. Let me."

She took the phone, swiped through options Maeve didn't recognize, selected something with a beat that sounded identical to the first one but was apparently completely different.

"This one's trending. You'll get more views."

"How do you know what's trending? You don't even have social media."

"Exactly. I know because I see what everyone else is posting. I just don't have to participate."

Maeve watched her daughter navigate the app with effortless fluency, adding text, adjusting timing, doing in thirty seconds what had taken Maeve twenty minutes.

"There. Posted."

"Thank you. I think."

Sage handed back the phone. "You know you're kind of addicted, right?"

"I'm not addicted. It's work."

"You check it like every five minutes."

"I have to. People message me with questions. Students need to book classes. It's how I run the business."

"Sure. But also you check it when you're watching TV. And at dinner. And at red lights."

Maeve opened her mouth to argue, then closed it.

She wasn't wrong.

That night, Maeve tried an experiment. She put her phone in a drawer after dinner and left it there.

For the first thirty minutes, she felt fine. Present. Engaged. She helped Finn with his Legos, actually looked at the tower he was building instead of glancing at it while scrolling.

By the forty-five minute mark, she was antsy. What if someone had messaged? What if there was a booking request she was missing? What if someone had commented something she needed to respond to?

By the hour mark, she'd made up an excuse to check it. "Just making sure no one cancelled tomorrow's class."

There were no cancellations. But there were seventeen notifications. She cleared them. Responded to a DM. Liked a few posts from students. Checked her insights. Noticed the reel Sage had fixed had 847 views—not bad —but the studio down the street had posted something similar with 3,000.

She went down the rabbit hole. Their page. Their reels. Their aesthetic. The cold plunge they'd just installed. The infrared sauna. The juice bar in the lobby.

Thirty minutes disappeared.

When she looked up, Finn had gone to bed. She'd missed saying goodnight.

"The fish doesn't know it's in the ocean," Maeve said to James later, on the lanai. "It just swims around looking for the thing it's already inside of."

"Is this about Instagram?"

"How did you know?"

"Because you've been weird about your phone all week. And you missed Finn's bedtime."

Maeve felt the sting of that. The guilt. She'd been right there, in the same house, and she'd still missed it.

"I don't know how to stop," she admitted. "It's my business. I have to be on there. But then I'm on there and I can't get off. And I'm comparing myself to every other studio, and they all have things I don't have, and I start thinking I need a cold plunge and a ring light and better abs—"

"You don't need better abs."

"That's not the point."

"What's the point?"

She stared at the sky. "The point is I'm drowning in something I'm supposed to be swimming in. The ocean isn't peaceful when you're exhausted. It's just wet and endless and you can't find the shore."

James considered this. "So stop swimming."

"I can't. If I stop posting, the algorithm buries me. If I stop engaging, people forget I exist. If I stop—"

"What if you just... posted less? Like, what you actually want to post, when you actually want to post it?"

"That's not how it works."

"Says who?"

"Says everyone. Every marketing guru, every social media expert, every—"

"Every fish who's also looking for the ocean?"

Maeve stopped. Looked at him.

"You've been doing this for fifteen years," James said. "Your studio is still here. Your students keep coming back. Not because of your reels. Because of you. Because of what happens in that room."

"But the new studios—"

"Will come and go. Some will succeed, most will fail. The ones that succeed won't succeed because of their Instagram. They'll succeed because they offer something real."

"What if I'm not enough? What if real isn't enough anymore?"

"Then nothing is. But I don't believe that. And I don't think you do either."

Maeve thought about Sage. Fourteen years old, no social media, and somehow more at peace with herself than Maeve had ever been at that age.

She'd asked Sage once why she didn't want Instagram. All her friends had it.

"Because it makes people crazy," Sage had said, with the clarity of someone who'd already figured out what took adults decades. "They're always comparing themselves. Always performing. Always wondering if they're good enough based on how many people liked their photo. That sounds exhausting."

"It is exhausting," Maeve had said.

"Then why do you do it?"

"Because I have to. For work."

Sage had just looked at her. That look teenagers give when they see through the excuse but are too tired to argue.

And she'd been right. Maeve didn't have to check Instagram during dinner. She didn't have to scroll through competitor accounts at midnight. She didn't have to measure her worth in likes and views and follower counts.

She chose to. Every time. She picked up the phone and dove back into the ocean, then complained about drowning.

The next morning, Maeve made a change.

She posted once—a simple photo of the studio, morning light, no reel, no trending audio, no hashtag strategy. Just: *Saturday morning. Doors open at 8. Come as you are.*

Then she put her phone in the drawer.

She taught her 9 a.m. class without checking it. Taught her 11 a.m. class without checking it. Had lunch with the kids—actually had lunch, actually tasted it, actually heard what they were saying—without checking it.

By 2 p.m., the itch was unbearable. But she noticed it instead of scratching it. Watched it pulse and fade and pulse again. Let it be uncomfortable.

At 4 p.m., she finally looked.

The simple post had forty-three likes. Fewer than usual. But four people had DM'd to say they loved it. That it felt real. That they were tired of the polished stuff and this was a breath of fresh air.

One message said: *This is why I come to your studio instead of the fancy new ones. You're not trying to be anything you're not.*

Maeve sat with that.

She'd been swimming in the ocean, searching for the ocean. Drowning in comparison while surrounded by enough. Scrolling through other people's content while ignoring her own actual life.

The young fish kept searching. But the ocean was already there. Had always been there. Would always be there.

She didn't have to find it.

She just had to stop looking and start feeling.

That night, the phone stayed in the drawer until the kids were in bed. She said goodnight to Finn. Read with Eli. Let Sage show her some video that was apparently hilarious for reasons Maeve didn't fully understand but laughed at anyway because Sage was laughing.

Later, on the lanai, she scrolled through the day's notifications. Cleared them without urgency. Responded to what needed responding. Ignored what didn't.

"Progress," James said, watching her put it away after ten minutes instead of forty.

"Baby steps."

"That's how you learn to swim."

"I thought the point was to stop swimming."

"The point is to remember you're already in the ocean. Then you can swim or float or just tread water. Whatever you want. But you stop panicking."

Maeve leaned back, looked at the stars. No screen between her eyes and the sky.

Sage didn't have social media and she was fine. Better than fine. She was present in a way Maeve had forgotten how to be.

The fancy new studios would keep opening. The reels would keep trending. The algorithm would keep changing. That was the ocean—constant, overwhelming, impossible to control.

But Maeve's studio was still here. Her students still came. The things that mattered couldn't be captured in a post.

She was swimming in it. She always had been.

Now she just had to remember.

16

The Stone Cutter

He wished to be the sun, then the cloud, then the wind, then the mountain—until he realized the stone cutter had been the most powerful all along.

There was once a stone cutter who was dissatisfied with his life.

Maeve stood at the front of the room, Monday evening, 6 p.m.—the after-work crowd, tired faces, sixteen students arranged on their mats.

"He looked up at the sun and wished he could be that powerful. And magically, he became the sun. He shone down on the earth, feeling invincible—until a cloud drifted by and blocked his rays. 'The cloud is more powerful than me,' he thought. So he wished to be a cloud."

She walked between the mats.

"As a cloud, he rained down on the earth, flooding fields, feeling mighty—until the wind blew him apart. 'The wind is more powerful,' he thought. So he became the wind. He howled across the land, bending trees, destroying houses—until he came to a mountain that wouldn't move. 'The mountain is more powerful.' So he became the mountain."

She returned to the front.

"He stood tall and immovable, certain that nothing could challenge him now—until he felt a sharp pain at his base. He looked down. A stone cutter was chipping away at him with a hammer and chisel. And the stone cutter realized: he had been the most powerful all along."

Maeve let the silence hold.

"We spend so much energy wishing we were something else. Someone else. Somewhere else. We look at others and think they have it figured out, they have the power, they have the answer. But the answer was always here. You were always enough. You just forgot."

She brought her hands to her heart.

"Let's begin."

The suggestion box had been James's idea.

"You're always wondering what people want," he'd said. "So ask them."

It had seemed so simple. A wooden box by the front desk, a stack of index cards, a pen on a string. Anonymous. Low stakes. Just a way to hear from students without putting them on the spot.

She'd emptied it for the first time that morning.

Twenty-three cards. She'd spread them across her desk like tarot, wondering what wisdom they'd reveal.

More hip openers please!

Fewer hip openers. My hips are open enough.

Can you play quieter music? It's distracting.

Can you play louder music? I can barely hear it.

The room is too hot.

The room isn't hot enough. This is supposed to be HOT yoga.

More spiritual stuff. I love the stories and the wisdom.

Less talking please. I just want to move.

Can we do more inversions?

I hate inversions. Can we skip them?

Your Tuesday teacher talks too much.

Your Tuesday teacher is my favorite. More classes with her please!

Maeve had stared at the cards. Twenty-three people. Twenty-three different versions of what the studio should be.

And then the last one, in handwriting she didn't recognize:

Have you considered offering more modern classes? The style feels a bit dated compared to other studios in town.

She'd read it three times. Dated. Her teaching was dated.

She'd been doing this for fifteen years. She'd trained

dozens of teachers. She'd built something real, something lasting, something that had survived a pandemic and competition and every trend that had come and gone.

And someone thought she was dated.

"Finn, you have to eat something."

Dinner. The nightly negotiation. Maeve stood at the counter, watching her five-year-old push spaghetti around his plate like it was a crime scene he was investigating.

"I'm not hungry."

"You haven't been hungry for three days. You have to eat."

"My tummy feels funny."

"Funny how?"

"Just funny."

The pediatrician's words echoed in her head. *He's in the 15th percentile for weight but the 85th for height. He's basically all vertical with nothing to sustain it. We need to get more calories into him.*

"What if I made you something else? Mac and cheese? A smoothie? Chicken nuggets?"

"I don't want chicken nuggets."

"You loved chicken nuggets yesterday."

"That was yesterday."

Sage looked up from her phone—a rare break from the no-phones-at-dinner rule, granted because she was researching something for a school project, allegedly. "Just let him not eat. He'll eat when he's hungry."

"The doctor said—"

"The doctor doesn't live here. If you force him, he'll just hate food more."

Maeve opened her mouth to argue, then closed it. When had her fourteen-year-old become the voice of reason?

"Fine. Finn, you don't have to eat the spaghetti. But you have to try three bites of something before you leave the table."

"Three bites of what?"

"Anything. Bread. Applesauce. Air. I don't care. Three bites."

Finn considered this. "Can I have ice cream?"

"Ice cream is not dinner."

"But it has calories."

Sage snorted. Eli, buried in a book as usual, didn't look up but was clearly smiling.

"Three bites of applesauce," Maeve said. "Then we can discuss ice cream."

"Deal."

He ate the applesauce in three enormous spoonfuls, declared himself finished, and ran off to play. Maeve looked at the untouched spaghetti, did the math on calories consumed versus calories needed, and decided not to think about it.

This was motherhood. The constant calculations no one warned you about. The calorie counts and the growth charts and the permission slips and the class snacks and the library books due and the soccer cleats that fit last month but don't fit now and the friend drama and the homework and the endless, endless logistics of keeping three small humans alive and fed and educated and emotionally regulated.

And that was before she got to the business. And the dogs. And the marriage.

The dogs.

Kona was old now—thirteen, gray-muzzled, arthritic. She spent most of her days on the orthopedic bed Maeve had bought her, watching the world with tired eyes. She'd been there since before the kids. Before the studio. She was the last remaining artifact of Maeve's twenties.

Mochi was anxious. Always had been, always would be. Thunder sent her into a spiral. Fireworks were a nightmare. She'd eaten three pairs of James's shoes and one corner of the couch during various panic episodes. But she was also the one who knew when Maeve was sad, who would press her golden head into Maeve's lap without being asked.

Beans was chaos. Pure, unfiltered, eight-month-old chaos. She'd chewed through two leashes, dug up the hibiscus, and figured out how to open the pantry door. Training was ongoing. Progress was questionable.

And then there was Poppy. The corgi. The one Maeve had wanted her whole life and finally let herself have.

Poppy was perfect—which somehow made her the most work. Because perfect dogs required perfect care, and Maeve was not a perfect owner. She was a tired owner who sometimes forgot the evening walk and sometimes fed kibble instead of the fancy raw food and sometimes fell asleep on the couch instead of doing the training exercises the YouTube videos said were essential.

Four dogs. Three kids. One husband. One business. One woman trying to hold it all together with caffeine and denial.

"The suggestion box was a mistake," Maeve said to James that night.

They were on the lanai. The kids were in bed—theoretically. Finn would probably appear in forty minutes with some excuse about bad dreams or thirst or the particularly haunting quality of the shadows in his room.

"Why? What did people say?"

"Everything. They said everything. More heat, less heat. More music, less music. More talking, less talking. One person said I'm dated."

"Dated?"

"Dated. My teaching style is dated."

James was quiet for a moment. "So one person out of how many?"

"Twenty-three."

"And the other twenty-two?"

"Mixed. Some loved things, some wanted changes. No consensus on anything."

"Sounds about right."

"It's frustrating. I wanted clarity. I wanted to know what people need so I could give it to them. Instead, I got confirmation that I can't please everyone."

"Did you think you could?"

Maeve sighed. "No. But I wanted to."

"That's the stone cutter."

"What?"

"The story you taught tonight. He kept wanting to be something else. The sun, the cloud, the wind. Always looking at the next thing, thinking it was more powerful. But he was already powerful. He just didn't see it."

"Are you saying I'm the stone cutter?"

"I'm saying you've been teaching yoga for fifteen years. You've built something real. People keep coming back. And one anonymous note about being 'dated' is making you question everything."

Maeve picked at a thread on her shorts. "It's not just the note. It's... I'm tired. I'm so tired. The studio, the kids, the dogs, the content creation, the—" She gestured vaguely at everything. "I feel like I'm doing a hundred things at sixty percent instead of ten things at a hundred percent."

"Welcome to parenthood."

"Is this it? Is this just what life is now? Running from thing to thing, never finishing anything, always behind?"

"For a while, yeah. The kids are young. The business is demanding. It won't always be this way."

"What if I can't wait that long?"

James didn't answer right away. He reached over, took her hand.

"You know what I see?" he finally said. "I see a woman who woke up at 5 a.m. to walk the dogs before the kids got up. Who made breakfast for three children with three different dietary requirements. Who taught two yoga classes while nursing a wrist injury. Who came home and helped with homework and negotiated a five-year-old into eating three bites of applesauce. Who cleaned up the kitchen and answered work emails and probably did fourteen other things I didn't even notice."

"That's just a Tuesday."

"Exactly. That's just a Tuesday. And you did it. You do it every day. The stone cutter was powerful, Maeve. He just forgot to look at his own hands."

Later that night, Finn appeared.

"Mama, I can't sleep."

Maeve looked at the clock. 10:47. Right on schedule.

"What's wrong, buddy?"

"My brain is too busy."

She scooted over, let him climb onto the bed. James grumbled but made room. The three of them lay there in the darkness, Finn's small body a furnace between them.

"What's your brain busy about?"

"I don't know. Everything. What if the sun explodes? What if Kona dies? What if I forget how to read?"

"Those are big worries."

"I have a big brain."

Maeve smiled in the dark. "You do. But here's the thing about big brains—they need rest. Even the biggest brains in the world have to sleep sometimes."

"What if I can't turn it off?"

"You don't have to turn it off. You just have to let the thoughts float by like clouds. You see them, but you don't grab them. You just let them pass."

"Like in yoga?"

"Exactly like in yoga."

Finn was quiet for a moment. Then: "Mama?"

"Yeah?"

"I'm glad you're my mom."

The words landed in her chest like a small, warm animal. All the exhaustion, all the frustration, all the suggestion box cards telling her she was too much or not enough—none of it mattered. This mattered. This small boy with his big brain and his busy thoughts, choosing her.

"I'm glad you're my kid."

"Even when I don't eat dinner?"

"Even when you don't eat dinner."

"Even when I wake you up at night?"

"Even then."

He snuggled closer. His breathing started to slow.

The stone cutter had wanted to be the sun. The cloud. The wind. The mountain. He'd traveled the whole world looking for power.

And power had been in his hands the whole time.

Maeve closed her eyes. Felt the weight of her son

against her side. Heard James's breathing settle into sleep.

The suggestion box could wait. The calories could wait. The content creation and the comparison and the endless running—all of it could wait.

Right now, she was exactly where she needed to be.

She was enough.

She slept.

17

The Raft
Use it to cross the river. Then set it down.

The Buddha told a parable about a man who needed to cross a river.

Maeve stood at the front of the room, Saturday morning, 9 a.m.—twenty students on their mats, the room warm, the energy expectant. She'd promised them something different today.

"There was no bridge, no boat, no way across. So he gathered logs and vines and built himself a raft. It took days. When it was finished, he used it to cross the river safely."

She walked between the mats.

"On the other side, he looked at the raft—this thing that had saved him, this thing he'd worked so hard to build—and he thought, 'This raft has been so useful. I should carry it with me in case I need it again.' So he hoisted it onto his shoulders and continued his journey, carrying the heavy raft wherever he went."

She returned to the front.

"The Buddha asked: Was this wise? The raft served its purpose. It got him across. But now it's just weight. Now it's slowing him down. The teaching is this: even helpful things must be set down once they've served their purpose. The raft that saves you can become the burden that sinks you—if you refuse to let it go."

Maeve paused, feeling the truth of it in her own body.

"Today, I want to try something different. Before we move, we're going to tap."

A few confused looks. A few knowing smiles.

"Some of you have heard of EFT—Emotional Freedom Technique. Tapping. It's a way of releasing stuck energy, stuck emotions, stuck patterns. You tap on specific points while acknowledging what you're carrying. It sounds strange. It looks stranger. But it works."

She demonstrated, tapping the side of her hand.

"We're going to tap out whatever raft you've been carrying. Whatever served you once but doesn't serve you now. Ready?"

She'd discovered tapping three years ago, during a particularly brutal stretch—the pandemic, the studio closed, the kids home, the walls closing in. A friend had sent her a YouTube video. "Just try it," she'd said. "I know it looks insane."

It did look insane. A woman tapping her face and collarbone while saying things like "Even though I feel overwhelmed, I deeply and completely accept myself."

Maeve had tried it anyway, alone in her bathroom, feeling ridiculous.

And something had shifted. Not dramatically. Not miraculously. But something. Like a valve releasing pressure she hadn't known was building.

She'd gotten certified online. Started doing it regularly. Started doing it on everyone.

The kids hated it.

"Mom, stop," Sage would say, pulling away when Maeve reached for her forehead.

"Just let me tap your karate chop point—"

"No. I'm fine. I don't need to be tapped."

Eli tolerated it with the weary patience of a middle child. He'd sit there, letting her tap his eyebrow and under his eye, waiting for it to be over.

Finn barely tolerated it. He'd squirm and giggle and say "that tickles" and run away after thirty seconds. But sometimes—sometimes—she'd catch him tapping his own collarbone when he was upset, and she'd know something had landed.

The dogs were easier. Mochi would lean into it, her anxious body softening as Maeve tapped along her spine. Kona would sigh and close her eyes. Beans would try to eat Maeve's fingers, which wasn't exactly the point but was at least engagement. Poppy would look at her with patient corgi judgment, as if to say, "I'll allow this, but I want you to know I find it undignified."

She'd tried tapping the guinea pigs once. They'd frozen, tiny hearts racing, clearly convinced this was a predator behavior. She'd stopped after ten seconds, apologized to them, and never tried again.

But the real test was the car.

She'd be driving, stuck in traffic, feeling the anxiety build—the running late, the mental to-do list, the weight of everything she wasn't getting done—and she'd start tapping. Side of the hand. Eyebrow. Side of the eye. Under the eye. Under the nose.

"Mom," Sage would hiss from the passenger seat. "Someone is looking at you."

"So?"

"So you look crazy. You're hitting yourself in the face at a red light."

"I'm not hitting myself. I'm tapping."

"That man can't look away. He's literally staring."

Maeve would glance over. Sure enough, someone in the next car would be watching, fascinated and horrified, as this woman in a minivan systematically tapped her face and muttered to herself.

She'd wave. They'd look away quickly, caught.

"You're embarrassing," Sage would say.

"I'm regulated," Maeve would reply. "There's a difference."

. . .

"Let's start with the side of the hand," Maeve said to the class. "This is the karate chop point. Tap here while you repeat after me."

Twenty adults, tapping the sides of their hands, waiting.

"Even though I'm carrying something heavy..."

"Even though I'm carrying something heavy," they echoed.

"Something that helped me once but doesn't help me now..."

"Something that helped me once but doesn't help me now..."

"I deeply and completely accept myself."

"I deeply and completely accept myself."

She moved them through the points. Eyebrow. Side of the eye. Under the eye. Under the nose. Chin. Collarbone. Under the arm. Top of the head.

"What are you ready to release?" she asked as they tapped. "What raft have you been carrying across dry land? A belief about yourself that protected you once but limits you now? A habit that got you through something hard but keeps you stuck? An identity that fit who you were but doesn't fit who you're becoming?"

She watched their faces. Some were crying. Some were laughing at the absurdity. Some were tapping with fierce concentration, clearly releasing something they'd been holding for years.

"You can tap out anything," she said. "Anger. Resentment. Fear. Grief. The stories you tell yourself about who you are and what you deserve. All of it can be released.

Not erased—we don't erase our experiences. But released. Set down. Like the raft."

That night, Maeve sat on the bathroom floor after the kids were in bed, tapping.

Side of the hand. "Even though I don't know what I'm supposed to let go of..."

Eyebrow. "Even though everyone says 'let go' like it's simple..."

Side of the eye. "And I don't know what that actually means..."

Under the eye. "I accept myself anyway."

She'd been thinking about this all day. The class had asked good questions. What do we let go of? How do we know when something has served its purpose? How do we set down the raft when the raft is who we think we are?

Under the nose. "I release the need to have it all figured out."

Chin. "I release the belief that I should be further along by now."

Collarbone. "I release the expectation that life should be easier than it is."

Under the arm. "I release the story that I'm not doing enough, being enough, giving enough."

Top of the head. "I release the raft of perfectionism that got me here but won't take me forward."

She sat with that one. Perfectionism. The raft she'd built so carefully, so long ago. The belief that if she just did everything right—the parenting, the teaching, the marriage, the business—she'd be safe. She'd be loved. She'd be enough.

It had served her once. It had driven her to build something real. To show up, day after day, even when she was tired. To hold herself to standards that most people wouldn't bother with.

But now?

Now it was just weight. Now it was the voice that said "dated" when one anonymous person criticized her. Now it was the calculation of Finn's calories that kept her up at night. Now it was the comparison to other studios, other mothers, other lives that looked shinier from the outside.

The raft had gotten her across the river. But she was still carrying it. And it was so, so heavy.

James found her on the bathroom floor.

"You okay?"

"I'm tapping."

"I can see that. On the bathroom floor?"

"The bathroom has good energy."

He sat down across from her, his back against the tub. "What are you tapping out?"

"Perfectionism. The need to have everything figured out. The belief that I should be further along."

"Further along to where?"

Maeve laughed. "I don't know. That's the problem. There's no destination. There's just this idea that wherever I am, I should be somewhere else. Whatever I'm doing, I should be doing it better. Whoever I am, I should be more."

"Says who?"

"The raft."

James looked at her. "You've lost me."

"The parable I taught today. A man builds a raft to cross a river. The raft saves him. But then he keeps carrying it, even on dry land, because it helped him once. Even though it's just weight now."

"And perfectionism is your raft."

"Perfectionism. Control. The belief that if I just try hard enough, nothing bad will happen." She tapped her collarbone absently. "It got me here. It built the studio. It made me a good teacher. But it's also the thing that keeps me up at night. That makes me feel like a failure when I'm actually doing fine. That tells me one critical comment matters more than a hundred good ones."

James was quiet for a moment. Then he reached over and tapped her on the forehead.

"What are you doing?"

"Tapping you. You tap everyone else. Dogs. Kids. Guinea pigs, apparently."

"The guinea pigs was a mistake."

"I'm tapping out your need to carry things alone." He moved to her eyebrow. "Your belief that asking for help is weakness." Side of her eye. "The story that you have to be everything to everyone." Under her eye. "The raft of martyrdom."

Maeve felt tears prick her eyes. "Martyrdom?"

"You do everything. You carry everything. And when someone offers to help, you say 'I've got it' like accepting help would prove you're not enough."

"That's not—" She stopped. Considered. "Okay. Maybe that's a little true."

"It's a lot true. And I get it. The raft got you here. But I'm here too. The kids are here. You don't have to carry everything alone anymore."

She leaned forward, rested her forehead against his shoulder.

"What if I don't know how to set it down?"

"Then you practice. Like everything else. You notice when you're carrying it. You choose to set it down. You pick it back up because that's what humans do. And then you set it down again."

"That sounds exhausting."

"Less exhausting than carrying a raft for the rest of your life."

The next morning, Maeve woke up before the alarm. Lay in the darkness, feeling the familiar pull—the mental list, the things to do, the weight of everything waiting for her.

She tapped her collarbone. Quietly, so she wouldn't wake James.

"I release the need to do it perfectly today. I release the belief that my worth depends on my productivity. I release the raft."

It didn't disappear. The list was still there. The weight was still there.

But it was lighter. Just slightly. Just enough.

She got up. Made coffee. Let the dogs out. Started the day.

The raft would be there when she needed it. She could pick it back up anytime.

But for today, just for today, she was going to try walking without it.

She was going to see how it felt to be light.

18

Hanuman
He forgot he could fly—until he remembered.

There is a story about Hanuman, the monkey god.

Maeve stood at the front of the room, Tuesday evening, 6 p.m.—fourteen students on their mats. Her voice was steady, but her life was not. Everything was in the air. Everything.

"As a child, Hanuman was mischievous and powerful. He leapt toward the sun, thinking it was a mango he could eat. The gods, alarmed by his power, struck him down with a thunderbolt. He fell to earth and forgot who he was. Forgot that he could fly. Forgot that he was divine."

She walked between the mats, feeling the weight of her own forgetting.

"Years later, when his beloved Rama needed him—when everything depended on Hanuman crossing an impossible ocean to find Sita—he stood at the shore, paralyzed. 'I can't do this,' he said. 'It's too far. I'm not strong enough.' And his friend Jambavan said: 'You have forgotten who you are. You are Hanuman. You can leap across oceans. You just have to remember.'"

She returned to the front.

"And Hanuman remembered. He grew to enormous size, leapt across the ocean, and saved everything that needed saving. Not because he gained new power—but because he remembered the power he already had."

Maeve brought her hands to her heart.

"Sometimes we forget we can fly. Fear makes us small. Doubt makes us forget. But the power is still there. We just have to take the leap—and trust that we'll remember mid-air."

She took a breath.

"Let's begin."

Two weeks.

They had two weeks until move-out, and nowhere to go.

The condo was nearly empty now—furniture sold or in storage, the kids' rooms echoing, the walls bare. They'd been sleeping on air mattresses for three days, living out of suitcases in their own home.

It had seemed like a good idea four months ago. The condo was too small. Three kids, four dogs, two adults—

they were bursting at the seams. The location wasn't great. The neighbors were loud. The HOA had sent them three letters about Beans barking.

"Let's sell," James had said. "Buy something bigger. A real house."

"We can't afford a real house in Anchor Bay."

"We can if we sell this first. Get top dollar. Use it as a down payment."

The math had worked on paper. Sell the condo, take the equity, buy the house. Simple.

Except to get top dollar, they had to stage it. And to stage it, they had to move out. And to move out, they needed somewhere to go.

"We'll find a short-term rental," Maeve had said. "Plenty of people do this."

There were not plenty of short-term rentals. There were almost none. And the ones that existed didn't allow pets—or charged astronomical fees for them. Four dogs was a dealbreaker everywhere.

They'd gone through the motions anyway. Listed the condo. Watched the showings happen. Got an offer—a good one. Accepted it.

And then the days started disappearing. Four weeks became three. Three became two.

"We could stay in a hotel," James said, not sounding like he believed it.

"With four dogs and three kids?"

"They have pet-friendly hotels."

"For four dogs? For weeks? Do you know what that would cost?"

"What choice do we have?"

Maeve didn't have an answer. She lay awake at night, running the numbers, trying to make them work. Hotel plus boarding for the dogs. Or an Airbnb an hour away, commuting to the studio. Or asking her mother, which wasn't really an option but kept surfacing anyway.

She second-guessed everything. Why had they done this? Why had they leapt before they knew where they'd land? The condo was fine. Small, but fine. They'd been safe there. Contained. And now everything was in storage and they were sleeping on air mattresses and she was teaching yoga classes about leaps of faith while privately falling apart.

One week before move-out, Maeve was lying on the air mattress at 3 a.m., staring at the ceiling.

The thought came from nowhere.

Check Craigslist.

She almost laughed. Craigslist? That was for scams and serial killers. Nobody found real housing on Craigslist anymore.

But the thought persisted. Not like her usual anxious thoughts, which spiraled and multiplied. This one was quiet. Steady. Like someone had placed it there.

Check Craigslist.

What the hell, she thought. What did she have to lose?

She pulled out her phone, navigated to the site—

when was the last time she'd even been on Craigslist?—and searched. Four bedroom. Pet friendly.

She wasn't even sure she was in the right region. The interface was confusing, dated, nothing like the slick apps she was used to.

The first listing stopped her.

4BR house, pet friendly, $2,800/month. Anchor Bay.

The price was wrong. Way too low. A four-bedroom in Anchor Bay for under three thousand? It had to be a scam. One of those fake listings designed to harvest your information.

But the thought came again: *What do you have to lose?*

She messaged the number. *Where are you located?*

The response came within minutes. An address. Two roads from Main Street. Two roads from the studio.

Can I see it?

Yes. Are you available now?

It was 3:47 a.m. Maeve stared at the phone.

How about 9am tomorrow?

That works.

She called James at 8:30, after school drop-off.

"I found something. On Craigslist."

"Craigslist?"

"I know. Just—can you meet me? 9 a.m. I'll send you the address."

The house was at the end of a quiet street. As they pulled up, Maeve saw water behind it. Actual water. A bay, stretching out blue and calm in the morning light.

"This can't be right," she said.

A woman was waiting on the porch. Sixty-something, gray hair, kind face. She introduced herself as Dorothy.

"My husband and I are moving to be closer to our grandchildren," she explained, unlocking the door. "We've owned this place for thirty years. Didn't want to sell—thought we might come back someday. So we're renting it. Just want someone who'll take care of it."

The inside was even better than the outside. Four bedrooms. A big kitchen. A living room with windows facing the water. A fenced backyard—actual grass, actual space for the dogs to run.

"You allow pets?" James asked, like he was waiting for the catch.

"How many do you have?"

"Four dogs. Three kids."

Dorothy smiled. "We had five dogs and four kids. This house can handle it."

Maeve walked through the rooms in a daze. This was real. This was actually real.

"The rent," she said. "The listing said $2,800?"

"That's right."

"That's... that's significantly below market."

"I know. I could charge more. But I don't need more. I need good tenants who'll love this place like we did."

Maeve looked at James. He looked at her.

"We'll take it," they said in unison.

. . .

They moved in the next morning. Lease signed, deposit paid, keys in hand.

The kids ran through the empty rooms, claiming bedrooms, discovering the backyard, shrieking about the water.

"There's a BEACH," Finn yelled. "We have a BEACH."

It wasn't exactly a beach—more of a rocky shoreline—but to a five-year-old, it was paradise.

The dogs explored every corner, tails wagging, finally having space to spread out. Poppy found a sunny spot by the window and claimed it immediately. Kona lowered herself onto the cool tile floor and sighed with what sounded like relief.

Maeve stood at the kitchen window, looking out at the bay. The studio was a seven-minute drive. The kids' schools were closer than before. The rent was less than their old mortgage.

It didn't make sense. None of it made sense.

"We were supposed to buy," she said to James. "That was the plan. Sell, buy, move once."

"Plans change."

"We're renters now. After fifteen years of owning, we're renters."

"Is that bad?"

She considered the question. They'd been so focused on the next step—the house they'd buy, the equity they'd build, the stability of ownership—that they'd almost missed this. A waterfront home for half of what they'd expected to pay. A year to breathe. A year to figure out what they actually wanted instead of what they thought they should want.

"No," she said slowly. "It's not bad. It's just... not what I expected."

"Hanuman didn't expect to fly, either. He just jumped and remembered mid-air."

Maeve laughed. "Have you been listening to my classes?"

"I'm always listening to your classes. Even when I'm pretending not to."

That night, after the air mattresses were inflated in their new rooms and the kids were finally asleep, Maeve walked down to the water's edge.

The bay was black and silver in the moonlight. She could hear the gentle lap of waves against the rocks. Somewhere across the water, lights from other houses glittered.

She'd been so afraid. So convinced that they'd made a terrible mistake. So certain that the leap would end in disaster.

And instead, it had ended here. In a house with a view. In a rent they could actually afford. In a life that looked different from the plan—but maybe better.

Check Craigslist.

The thought had come from somewhere. Nowhere. The place where nudges live—the ones that don't feel like yours, the ones that turn out to be exactly what you needed.

She'd almost ignored it. Almost let her certainty that it couldn't work stop her from finding out if it could.

Hanuman had forgotten he could fly. He'd stood at the ocean's edge, paralyzed by the distance, convinced he wasn't strong enough.

But he'd jumped anyway. And mid-air, he'd remembered.

Maeve looked up at the moon—the same moon Ryokan had wanted to give the thief, the same moon that couldn't be stolen.

She'd taken the leap. She'd landed somewhere unexpected.

And for the first time in months, she felt like she could breathe.

She walked back up to the house. Checked on each sleeping child. Let the dogs out one more time. Stood at the kitchen window, looking at her new view.

Tomorrow there would be boxes to unpack. A condo sale to close. A life to rebuild in this new space.

But tonight, she could just be here. In the house that Craigslist found. In the life that wasn't the plan but might be the answer.

She'd jumped.

She'd remembered how to fly.

19

Ganesha
The remover of obstacles is also the placer of obstacles.

Ganesha is the elephant-headed god. The remover of obstacles.

Maeve stood at the front of the room, Thursday morning, 9 a.m.—eighteen students on their mats. Her wrist was wrapped in a brace she barely noticed anymore.

"But here's what most people don't know," she said. "Ganesha doesn't just remove obstacles. He also places them. He puts things in our path—not to punish us, but to teach us. The obstacle isn't in the way. The obstacle is the way."

She walked between the mats.

"Every challenge you're facing right now—the thing

that feels like it's blocking you, stopping you, making your life harder—what if it's not a problem to be solved? What if it's a teacher? What if the obstacle is exactly what you need to become who you're meant to be?"

She returned to the front, flexing her fingers experimentally.

"Speaking of obstacles. Some of you have noticed I've been modifying. My wrist—" she held it up— "decided to teach me something. It's been months now, and it's not healing the way I expected. The doctor says I may never do a full weight-bearing chaturanga again."

A murmur of sympathy rippled through the room.

"At first, I was devastated. Chaturanga is fundamental. It's in every vinyasa. How could I teach yoga if I couldn't do the most basic transition?"

She paused, smiled.

"But here's what I discovered. I found a new way. I've been using my fingers differently, distributing weight through my knuckles instead of my palms, modifying the angle. And you know what? I feel stronger. Not despite the limitation—because of it. The obstacle forced me to find something I never would have looked for."

She demonstrated—a modified chaturanga, fingers spread wide, weight shifted, elbows tracking differently.

"I'm not doing traditional chaturangas anymore. Probably ever. And I've made peace with that. I hated them anyway."

Laughter. And then—

"Oh thank god," someone in the back row said. Loudly.

More laughter. Then a chorus:

"I hate them too."

"They hurt my shoulders."

"I've been dreading them for years."

"Can we all stop doing them?"

Maeve grinned. "Here's the thing—you never had to do them. You could always modify. You could always do knees-chest-chin, or skip it entirely, or find your own version. But you thought you had to. You thought there was a right way and a wrong way, and chaturanga was the right way."

She looked around the room.

"There is no right way. There's only your way. The obstacle isn't the pose. The obstacle is the belief that you have to do it like everyone else."

She brought her hands to her heart.

"Let's begin. And today—no chaturangas. For anyone. Let's see what else is possible."

Linda came back to the studio three weeks after her surgery.

She moved slowly. Carefully. Nothing like the woman who used to flow through class with quiet confidence. She walked like someone learning to trust her body again.

"I can't do a real class yet," she said, standing in Maeve's office doorway. "But I can't stay home anymore either. I'm going crazy."

"What do you need?"

"I don't know. Something gentle. Just... movement. Breath. Proof that I'm still alive."

They started meeting on Tuesday afternoons. Just the two of them, in the empty studio between classes. No agenda. No sequence. Just Linda's body telling Maeve what it needed, and Maeve listening.

Some days they just breathed. Sat on bolsters and practiced inhaling, exhaling, feeling the lungs expand against the ribs. Linda would cry sometimes—not from sadness, but from the strangeness of being back in a body that had betrayed her and saved her in the same moment.

"They cracked my chest open," she said during one session, lying in supported fish pose, a bolster under her spine. "They stopped my heart. Put me on a machine. Fixed the valve. Started my heart again. And now I'm just supposed to... go back to normal?"

"There's no normal after something like that."

"Then what is there?"

"There's this. Right now. Your heart beating. Your lungs breathing. You, alive, on this mat."

Linda closed her eyes. Tears slid down her temples.

"I went to Paris," she said. "Before the surgery. You told me to taste the strawberry."

"I remember."

"It was the best trip of my life. My daughter and I— we ate croissants every morning. We walked until our feet hurt. We sat by the Seine and just... watched the world go by. I kept thinking, if this is my last week, it's a good one."

"And it wasn't your last week."

"No. It wasn't." Linda opened her eyes, looked at the ceiling. "But I'm different now. I don't know how to be the person I was before. She didn't know her heart could stop. I do."

Maeve didn't try to fix it. Didn't offer platitudes about everything happening for a reason. She just sat with Linda in the truth of it—the before and the after, the body that had been broken open and was slowly learning to hold itself together again.

"The obstacle is the way," Maeve said quietly.

"What?"

"Something I taught this morning. Ganesha. He places obstacles in our path—not to stop us, but to change us. Your heart wasn't just a problem to be fixed. It was a teacher."

Linda was quiet for a long moment. Then: "A really painful teacher."

"The best ones usually are."

***

The call from Eleanor's nephew came on a Wednesday.

Maeve saw the unfamiliar number, felt her stomach clench. She'd been waiting for this for weeks—ever since the property management company had mentioned the estate, the transition, the nephew named David who would be handling things.

"Ms. Campbell? This is David Matsuda. Eleanor's nephew."

"Yes. Hello."

"I wanted to call you personally. I know my aunt thought highly of you."

Maeve braced herself. Here it came. The rent increase. The sale. The end of everything she'd built.

"I've been going through her papers," David continued. "She kept a file on every tenant. Yours was... extensive. Letters from students. Photos from events. A newspaper clipping from when you reopened after the pandemic."

"She came to the reopening. Wore one of her scarves."

"That sounds like her." He paused. "Ms. Campbell, I'm calling to tell you that I'm not changing anything. Your rent stays the same. Your lease terms stay the same. Eleanor believed in you, and I'm honoring that."

Maeve sat down. Her legs had stopped working.

"I—thank you. I don't know what to say."

"You don't have to say anything. Just keep doing what you're doing. That's what she would have wanted."

After she hung up, Maeve sat in her office for a long time. The studio was quiet. The afternoon light slanted through the windows.

Eleanor was gone. But her belief lived on. Her nephew, a stranger, had chosen to honor it.

Some obstacles never materialized. Some fears turned out to be phantoms. And sometimes, the universe just... gave you a break.

"Mom, there's a trip."

Eli was standing in the kitchen doorway, permission slip in hand. He'd been hovering for ten minutes, waiting for the right moment. Classic Eli—never wanting to interrupt, never wanting to be a bother.

"What trip?"

"Washington DC. With my grade. It's five days. We'd see the monuments and the Smithsonian and the Capitol building and—"

"How much?"

He hesitated. "Eighteen hundred dollars."

"Eighteen hundred dollars?"

"Plus spending money. So maybe two thousand total."

Maeve's first instinct was automatic. No. Too expensive. Unnecessary. He didn't need to go to Washington DC. He could learn about the monuments from books.

The word was already forming in her mouth when she stopped.

She looked at Eli. Really looked at him.

When was the last time he'd asked for anything? Sage asked for everything—new makeup, concert tickets, clothes she'd wear once. And Maeve usually found a way to say yes, because Sage asked so persistently that it was easier to give in than to keep fighting.

Finn got something every time they went to Target. A small toy, a pack of stickers, a candy bar. It had become ritual. He expected it now.

But Eli? Eli never asked. Eli saw the credit card bill on the counter and quietly put back the book he'd been holding. Eli wore shoes that were too small because he didn't want to mention that his feet had grown. Eli was the one who said "I'm fine" when asked what he wanted for his birthday, and meant it, because he'd learned that wanting things led to disappointment.

She'd done this to him. Not on purpose. But she'd done it. She'd rewarded the squeaky wheels and ignored the quiet one, and now her middle child had learned that his needs didn't matter.

"When is it?" she asked.

"April. But we have to sign up by next week to hold a spot."

"And you want to go?"

His face flickered—hope and wariness, like an animal that had been tricked before. "I mean, it sounds cool. But I know it's a lot of money. If we can't—"

"We can."

He stared at her. "What?"

"We can. I'll figure it out. You should go."

"But you said—"

"I didn't say anything yet. I was about to say something dumb, but I stopped myself." She walked over, took the permission slip from his hands. "You never ask for anything, Eli. And that's not a good thing. It means I haven't been paying attention. So yes. You're going to Washington DC."

His eyes went bright. He blinked rapidly, looking away.

"Thanks, Mom."

"Don't thank me. Just—next time you want something, tell me. Okay? Don't assume the answer is no."

He nodded. Grabbed an apple from the counter—that was Eli, always taking care of himself, never asking anyone else to do it—and headed for his room.

Maeve looked at the permission slip. Eighteen hundred dollars. They didn't have eighteen hundred dollars sitting around. Not with the move, the storage unit, the new rental deposit.

But she'd find it. She'd figure it out. Because Eli deserved a trip to Washington DC. Eli deserved to be seen.

The obstacle wasn't the money. The obstacle was her automatic no. The pattern she'd fallen into without realizing—saying yes to the ones who demanded and no to the one who didn't.

Ganesha had placed that obstacle in her path. And she'd finally seen it.

That night, Maeve sat on the new porch—their porch now, the one that faced the water—and watched the moon rise over the bay.

So many threads resolving. Linda healing. Eleanor's nephew honoring her legacy. Eli getting his trip. The wrist becoming a teacher instead of a tragedy.

"Good day?" James asked, settling into the chair beside her.

"Yeah. Actually. A really good day."

"That's allowed, you know. Good days."

"I'm learning."

She told him about David's call. About signing Eli up

for DC. About the class that had collectively celebrated the death of chaturanga.

"Wait—no more chaturangas? Ever?"

"Not for me. The students can do what they want. But I'm done."

"And people were happy about this?"

"Thrilled. It turns out everyone's been suffering through them for years, waiting for permission to stop."

James laughed. "So your injury freed everyone."

"Apparently."

She flexed her wrist. It still ached sometimes. Probably always would. But she'd found a new way. A different way. Not better, not worse—just hers.

"Ganesha," she said.

"The elephant god?"

"The placer of obstacles. I taught about him today. How the things that block us are actually teaching us. How the obstacle is the way."

"And you believe that?"

Maeve considered the question. The wrist that had forced her to change. The suggestion box that had taught her she couldn't please everyone. The friend who'd walked away and taught her about carrying. The leap of faith that had landed them here, on this porch, looking at this water.

"I'm starting to," she said. "Not in a magical thinking way. Not like everything happens for a reason. More like—the things that go wrong show us who we are. They strip away the stuff that doesn't matter. They make us figure out what does."

"That's pretty wise."

"I'm pretty wise. I'm a yoga teacher. It's in the job description."

James reached over, took her hand.

They sat in the quiet, watching the moon climb higher. The bay was silver and black, the water lapping softly against the rocks.

Tomorrow there would be more obstacles. More things that went wrong, more plans that shifted, more lessons she hadn't asked for.

But tonight, she could just sit here. In the house that wasn't the plan. With the wrist that had changed her teaching. With the middle child who was going to Washington DC.

Ganesha had placed a lot of obstacles in her path this year.

And every single one had been a teacher.

20

Chop Wood, Carry Water

Before enlightenment, chop wood, carry water. After enlightenment, chop wood, carry water.

A student traveled for years searching for enlightenment.

Maeve stood at the front of the room, Saturday morning, 9 a.m.—her last class of the year. The room was full. The seasonal yogis were there—Barbara and Stan, the Hendersons, Michael. The regulars were there—the ones who'd been coming for years, the ones who'd started just this month. Linda was there, in the second row, three months post-surgery, moving gently but moving.

"He climbed mountains," Maeve said. "He studied with masters. He fasted and meditated and read every sacred text he could find. Finally, after years of seeking, he found a teacher who looked at him and said: 'You're ready. You've achieved enlightenment.'"

She walked between the mats.

"The student was overjoyed. 'What do I do now?' he asked. 'Now that I'm enlightened, how does my life change?'"

She returned to the front.

"The teacher smiled and said: 'Before enlightenment, chop wood, carry water. After enlightenment, chop wood, carry water.'"

She let the silence hold.

"Nothing changes. Everything changes. You still wake up early. You still make breakfast and pack lunches and forget where you put your keys. You still teach the same classes, parent the same children, walk the same dogs. The tasks don't change. But you change. You're the same person doing the same things—but you're doing them awake. You're doing them with presence. You're doing them knowing that this—all of this—is the practice."

She brought her hands to her heart.

"This is our last class of the year. I want to thank you for showing up. For trusting me with your bodies and your breath and your Saturday mornings. For teaching me—" her voice caught slightly— "even when you didn't know you were teaching."

She took a breath.

"Let's begin."

. . .

The class was simple.

No complicated sequences. No peak poses. Just breath and movement, the basics, the things she'd been teaching for fifteen years. Sun salutations. Standing poses. A long, slow cool-down. A savasana that stretched longer than usual because no one wanted to leave.

Maeve moved through the room, adjusting, cueing, watching.

There was Diane, still arriving late, still unrolling her mat like a sacred scroll while everyone else held their breath. But Maeve saw her differently now. Saw the single mother who'd rushed from her night shift, who came even when she was exhausted, who needed this room more than anyone knew.

There was Tom, the former athlete, still treating every pose like competition. But she saw him now—the fear beneath the striving, the man who didn't know who he was if he wasn't winning. He was learning. Slowly. They all were.

There was the woman who cried in hip openers. She was crying now, tears sliding down her temples into her hair. Maeve didn't know her story—she'd never asked, never needed to. Some things didn't need words. Some things just needed space.

There was Linda, moving through gentle modifications, her hand occasionally drifting to her chest. She'd gone to Paris. She'd had the surgery. She was here. That was its own kind of miracle.

"Begin to deepen your breath," Maeve said, bringing

them out of savasana. "Invite movement back into your fingers and toes. Feel yourself returning to the room."

She watched them stir. Twenty-two bodies, twenty-two lives, twenty-two sets of obstacles and lessons and ordinary miracles.

"When you're ready, roll to your right side. Take a moment there. The fetal position—where we all began."

She gave them time. Didn't rush.

"Press yourself up to seated. Let your head be the last thing to rise."

They rose, one by one, finding their seats, finding their breath.

"Bring your hands together at your heart."

Twenty-two pairs of hands. Twenty-two hearts beating beneath them.

"Thank you for your practice," Maeve said. "Thank you for this year. Thank you for teaching me."

She bowed her head.

"Namaste."

After class, students lingered longer than usual.

Barbara hugged her tight. "Same time next December?"

"Same time next December."

"You've changed," Barbara said. "This year. I don't know how, but you're different."

"Good different or bad different?"

"Just... more you. More here."

Maeve didn't know what to say to that. So she just hugged her again.

Linda was last to leave.

"I almost didn't go to Paris. You know that? I almost let fear win. But I kept thinking about the strawberry. And the moon. And all the things that can't be stolen." She smiled. "You probably don't remember saying any of that."

"I remember."

"It mattered. All of it. More than you know."

She squeezed Maeve's hand and walked out into the morning light.

Maeve stood in the empty studio. The mats were still warm. The room still smelled like sweat and essential oils and something harder to name—effort, maybe. Or hope.

She thought about what Barbara had said. *You're different. More you. More here.*

Was that enlightenment? Not some dramatic transformation, not a bolt of lightning or a moment of cosmic clarity. Just... more here. More awake. More present in the chopping of wood and the carrying of water.

She started cleaning. Sprayed the mats. Wiped down the props. Straightened the bolsters against the wall.

Chop wood. Carry water.

The same tasks she'd done after every class for fifteen years. But different now. Lighter. More hers.

That night, the house was chaos.

Finn wouldn't eat dinner. "My tummy feels funny."

"Your tummy always feels funny. Three bites."

"Of what?"

"Anything. Air. I don't care."

Sage was upset about something she wouldn't explain, locked in her room with music playing loud enough to shake the walls.

Eli needed help with a project due Monday that he'd known about for three weeks.

The dogs needed walking. The dishes needed doing. The laundry had been sitting in the dryer for two days.

Maeve moved through it all.

Three bites negotiated (applesauce, always applesauce). Sage's door knocked on, not forced open, just letting her know she was there when she was ready. Eli's project half-finished, the rest bookmarked for tomorrow. Dogs walked in the dark, flashlight in one hand, leashes tangled in the other.

Before enlightenment, chop wood, carry water.

After enlightenment, chop wood, carry water.

Nothing had changed. She was still tired. Still stretched thin. Still counting bites and checking on teenagers and searching for matching socks.

But something had changed too. Something she couldn't name but could feel.

She wasn't fighting it anymore. Wasn't wishing she were somewhere else, someone else, in some other life where things were easier. This was her life. These were her people. This was the practice.

Not the yoga on the mat. The yoga of Tuesday night

laundry and Sunday morning pancakes and the endless, exhausting, miraculous work of keeping people alive and loved.

Later, after the kids were finally asleep and James was reading and the dogs were arranged in their various spots around the house, Maeve went outside.

The bay was black and silver. The moon was full—round and bright, impossibly beautiful.

She thought about the year.

Muddy water. Second arrows. Leaking buckets. Strawberries between tigers. Monks and scorpions. Stone cutters and rafts. Fish in oceans they couldn't see. Hanuman remembering mid-leap that he could fly.

She'd taught every one of those lessons. And every one of those lessons had taught her.

When the student is ready, the teacher appears.

She'd been looking for the teacher everywhere—in books, in trainings, in the wisdom of people who seemed to have it figured out.

And the teacher had been there all along. In her own words. In her own students. In the mirror of her own teaching.

She was the student.

She was the teacher.

She was both. She had always been both.

. . .

The next morning, Maeve woke before the alarm.

5 a.m. The house was quiet. Even the dogs were still asleep.

She made coffee. Let Kona out—slowly, carefully, the old dog's joints stiff with age. Stood at the window watching the bay turn pink with sunrise.

Today there would be classes to teach. Kids to feed. Dogs to walk. A husband to love. A life to live.

The same life. The same tasks. The same chopping of wood and carrying of water.

But she was different now. Not transformed—just awake. Not enlightened in any dramatic sense—just present. Finally present for the life she'd been living all along.

She thought about what she'd tell her students today. What parable, what lesson, what truth disguised as a story.

And she realized: it didn't matter. Whatever she taught would be what she needed to learn. Whatever she offered would be what she needed to receive. That was how it worked. That was how it had always worked.

The student and the teacher were the same person.

The obstacle and the path were the same thing.

The practice wasn't separate from the life. The practice WAS the life.

She finished her coffee. Woke the kids. Started the day.

Chop wood.

Carry water.

Begin again.

The End

ABOUT THE AUTHOR

About the Author

Niki Robinson Ague is the owner and main instructor of Hot Yoga by the Sea in Kailua, Hawaii, which she opened in 2010. She teaches approximately fifteen yoga classes per week across various styles including hot yoga, vinyasa flow, yin yoga, yoga nidra, breathwork, and sound healing.

Much of what she wrote in *Off the Mat* mirrors her own life—the chaos of motherhood, the juggle of running a small business, the lessons that find you whether you're ready or not. Maeve's story is fiction, but the texture is real: the five-year-old who won't eat, the teenager who cringes at your music choices, the dogs who need tapping, the husband who listens even when he pretends not to, and the students who become family.

Niki is also the author of *Finding Shanti*, *The Complete Yoga Nidra Book*, *Flow Foundations*, *Soul Dog*, and several other titles available on Amazon.

For more real, honest, and raw life experiences as a yogi mom, follow her daily podcast **Off the Mat** on Spotify.

www.hotyogabythesea.com

Made in the USA
Coppell, TX
15 February 2026

72017936R00157